An Honorable Man:

The Romance of Cluny Ramm

I0620430

ED PEOPLES

by

Ed Peoples

Published by Meadow Crest Publishing
Forestville, CA 95436
meadowcrestpublishing@msn.com

This is a work of fiction. However, one real character, a musician, is included in one scene and several other musicians are mentioned. Otherwise, names, characters, places, and incidents either are the product of the author's imagination or repressed memory, or are a combination of known characters used factiously and any other resemblance to actual persons, living or dead, events, or locales is entirely coincidental. However, the actual names of certain towns and other locations, and of certain public figures are used within the context of the fiction

This book is dedicated to Music,
for music tenderizes the spirit and brings aid
and comfort to the soul

Acknowledgments

The author would like to thank Arlene Miller, the Grammar Diva for her valuable help in copy editing this work.

The author would also like to thank Craig Taylor Peoples for his sharp eye and keen sense of word usage and content.

Dix was told that he would have to take the LSAT exam given by the testing service from Princeton, New Jersey and receive a qualifying score before admission. He could take that test the first Saturday of each month there at the College. The fee to take the exam was $25, and there was a $10 application fee to the College. Once admitted and enrolled, the fee for each course would be $25 per unit.

He could choose between two degree options: three years full time or four years part time, or some combination thereof. Day classes were offered throughout each day, Monday through Friday, and evening classes were offered Monday through Thursdays from four to seven p.m. and seven to ten p.m.

Dix took applications for both admission and the LSAT exam, and said that he was considering a legal career and would think over what she had said. The receptionist gave him a brochure to read which offered all the details and procedures to follow. He thanked the receptionist and left. The course requirements felt like an overload on his brain. Why would he want to take that on?"

How quickly life's direction can change, Dix thought. Only this morning he was considering the possibility of buying the hardware store in Ultumia and settling there forever. He knew that clerking in a store might not be his thing. He might be bored out of his skull. It lacked activity, which Dix needed, but he had been caught up in the idea of changing jobs, or leaving the justice system behind with all its many frustrations and few rewards. A country store might be just the diversion he needed. However, now he was excited about the possibility of working within the system, but as an attorney, and having an impact on the poor and misbegotten souls whose lives were sucked into the system by the disparity and dysfunctions inherent in the bureaucracy and in their own lives.

Dix was aware that his life was becoming more complicated and that he had several career options from which to choose.

First, he needed to check with Holly about their plans for Wednesday. He also had to meet with Judge Jones today at some point. And he wanted to stop by Ross Jewelry in Riverton to check on prices for an engagement ring.

He decided to return to the office and take care of the first two items before he left for the day. He parked near the back door in one of the public parking places that had a maximum of one-hour parking.

Dix went right to his desk. First, he called Judge Jones' chambers and made an appointment to see the Judge. The clerk, Mrs. Butler, said that the Judge had told her he was expecting my call and that he was available anytime this afternoon. They arranged for a meeting for two p.m.

Next, Dix phoned Holly. She confirmed that all was well and as arranged. She would see him Tuesday morning.

Dix had an hour to kill while waiting for his meeting with the Judge, so he opened his field book and thumbed through it to see what cases needed his attention and whom he should contact first.

Dix entered the outer office to Judge Jones' chambers just two minutes before the appointed hour. Mrs. Butler looked from her desk and smiled.

"Ah, Mr. Monroe. The Judge is expecting you. Please go right in."

Dix entered the chambers, not knowing what to expect. Judge Jones was hunched over his desk reading some case file. He rose and came around the desk, and held out his hand.

"Mr. Monroe. So good of you to come. I know that we are both busy people, so I'll come right to the point. I liked the way you handled yourself in the situation that arose during arraignment this morning. I would like you to attend my arraignment calendar every Monday and assume the role of a facilitator, as it were. I can't rely on any of the attorneys to assist in that manner. They're too busy with their own cases. You know what cases are relevant to probation, and you have that likeable but controlling manner that can handle most any situation that might arise. I don't expect a repeat of Mrs. Lamarr's confrontation this morning, but one never knows what might happen from week to week. Arraignment during the rest of the week is light and doesn't present the same potential for problems. I know that you indirectly serve as an arm of the court. That is, your chief is a judicial appointment and serves at the pleasure of the court. You don't, at least not directly. I don't want to lean on you, but I can clear this with your chief, and it would be a part of your regular probation workload."

"Your honor, I'm at a loss for words. I appreciate your favorable assessment of my behavior in the court, and I must say, I did enjoy being the facilitator, as you called it."

"Give it some thought and let me know. I would greatly appreciate your presence like that in the courtroom."

"Well, your Honor, I'm not one to waste time mulling over an issue when the response is obvious to me. If you clear it with the Chief, I'll be there Monday morning. I look forward to it."

"That was a quick decision, but then I see you as a decisive person who quickly knows his own mind and acts accordingly. That is what I want in my courtroom. Mr. Monroe, I thank you."

And the Judge rose and held out his hand again. They shook, as if sealing the deal.

"While I have your ear Judge," said Dix, "I would like your advice on another matter."

"Yes, by all means. I always like giving other people advice."

"I am considering applying for law school at McBrown. I'd like to hear your thoughts on the idea."

"McBrown has a fine program. It's new and has a first-rate faculty. I should know because I am one of the founders of the College and one of the faculty in the evening program. Judges Raskin and Temple are also on the part-time staff. I think you would make a great attorney. I can just see you in the court room, slaying all the dragons and tilting at all the windmills to bring about justice."

"I supposed I might have seemed over-zealous in your court today, and I will admit that I enjoyed the scene.'

"Unfortunately, justice is not clear-cut and is seldom achieved. You should be aware that as a criminal defense attorney you will not be working to get the innocent and downtrodden freed from an unjust situation. Most of the time you will be defending guilty people. Actually, you will not be defending people, but you will be defending the rights guaranteed to everyone under the Constitution. Consequently, your first line of attack will be at the police procedures that yielded an arrest. Was there reasonable suspicion to make a stop or a detention. Was there probably cause for the arrest or make a search. You'll have the police officers on the stand, grilling them to find the illegal hole in their procedures. From your point of view, it will be the police behavior that is on the stand, not the behavior of an accused. Of course, if you can see that the police procedures were legal and the other evidence is sound, you'll work with the prosecuting attorney to make the best deal for your client. If all those efforts fail, then you just might go on to trial. In that case, you will work on the jury to create doubt, a reasonable doubt in the mind of at least one juror. If those are the aspects of the role of a defense attorney appeal to you, then be all mens go to law school."

"Judge, your description of the job is not what I had in mind. I guess I was being naive. At least I have a more complete picture to consider in coming to a decision. Thank you very much. I'll let you know. And, I'll be in your courtroom next Monday morning."

Dix had an entirely new perspective on the role of a defense attorney. It made his decision more realistic, but more complicated.

Dix left Judge Jones' chambers in a state of mixed, but emotions. He didn't like the idea of having to commit to be in the arraignment court every Monday, yet he enjoyed the accolades given him by the judge, and he looked forward to his role as facilitator. It was as if he had auditioned for the lead role in a courtroom drama and had been given the part. What a grand opportunity. But is what he would be preparing for something that he now wanted?

Dix checked out with the probation department's front desk, saying again that he was going out into the field for the rest of the day. Then he drove to Riverton and stopped at Ross Jewelry on Main Street.

Ross had an array of diamond engagement rings displayed in the front window. They were all sizes and prices. He entered the store and looked at the additional rings in the display cases until Mr. Ross came over and waited on him.

"What may I help you find today?" Ross asked.

"I'm not sure what I want. My situation is this: I am going to propose to a woman soon, but I want her to choose the ring and get it fitted. That is, if she says yes. However, I need something of offer her when I propose."

"I know just what you mean. We often have men coming in here under the same circumstance. I have the solution."

Ross reached behind the display case and came out with a nice-looking diamond in a gold setting. "This is our least expensive ring and setting, but it is one that we suggest you take to offer during your proposal. Once it is accepted, you immediately explain that it is merely a token ring, but that you want her to come with you to choose the one that she wants. The one that will last her a lifetime."

"That is just the solution I am looking for. I can see that I am not the first one to be in this situation. But can she wear this one for a day or two until we come in? I know that she will want to show it off to family and friends."

"Absolutely. Notice that the band is open at the bottom and can easily be adjusted for temporary use. What I will need from you is some personal and financial information on yourself and a deposit of $50. Then you take this ring in this nice case and offer it as you propose. The two of you can make an appointment to come in for a sizing and selection of her ring. You will have thirty days from today to complete the selection, and the $50 will apply toward the final purchase. After the thirty days, you have bought yourself that ring for $50."

Dix gave Ross all the information he required, along with the deposit, and left the store. He felt committed now, and also felt a flash of anxiety in the pit of this stomach.

He phoned Cluny at the inn.

"Hi Dix, I was hoping you would call, but tonight is developing into a busy time. We're over-booked for dinner because some of our weekend guests decided to stay over a few more days. I can't get away.""

"I'll miss you. Call you tomorrow. Love you."

"Love you too. Bye."

Chapter Twenty-Two

It was Tuesday morning, and Dix was still basking in the night of loving with Cluny on Sunday. He didn't want to break the spell, as it were, but he did have to meet with Holly Trent and her CBI associate in Vacaville.

He took Adobe Road out of the southeast side of Riverton and caught Highway 12 just south of Sonoma. He drove east on 12 past the south end of Napa to intersect with Highway 80, toward Vacaville and the Coffee Tree. As he drove by Vacaville, the strong aroma of onions filled the air from the nearby onion processing plant, and his olfactory receptors turned on to high alert. He began to crave a cheeseburger.

Dix had figured on an hour-and-a-half drive. Traffic was light, and he arrived at the Coffee Tree Restaurant early, at about nine-thirty. He was seated inside next to a window looking out onto the parking lot.

The waitress came and left a menu. A nametag with the name Chris was pinned to her blouse. She was a cute and petite redhead with and a friendly smile. "Hi, Chris, there will be two more for breakfast."

"Do I know you?" she asked.

"No, I don't think so."

"Well you called me by name, and I thought I should know you."

"Oh, I read your name off of that name tag." Dix pointed to her blouse.

Chris blushed. She wasn't expecting that, and she was flustered. "May I get you some coffee?"

"Sure. Black please."

Holly Trent and her agent associate arrived fifteen minutes later. Dix watched them walk to the restaurant from their car. They both were about five feet eight, but he was heavyset, wearing black leather pants and a purple herringbone shirt with puffy sleeves and a black leather vest, while she wore a brown hearing bone skirt; white blouse, and blue cashmere sweater. Her hair was dyed blond. He lumbered along and she had a brisk deliberate step. What a pair, Dix thought.

Once inside the door, Holly scanned inside the restaurant as they entered. She spotted Dix right away and went to his table, smiling and holding out her arms for a hug.

Dix watched her walked toward the table. She was a little heavier than he remembered, about five foot-eight, 140 pounds now, and when she drew near, he could see some gray streaks in her short, bobbed hair, and crow's feet were beginning to show around her eyes.

Dix rose from his chair to greet her, and they hugged like old friends would.

"Dix, I would have recognized you anywhere, but you have changed. You're all beefed up and you look more mature than I remember."

To Dix, that meant that he was looking older too. He could have told her that she looked more mature as well, but he didn't.

"Holly, you look wonderful. It's so good to see you."

She motioned to her associate and introduced him. "This is Armund Hernandez, Special Agent with CBI."

They shook hands and exchanged greetings. Hernandez was Latino, a chubby five feet seven, with long, flowing black hair and an exotic-looking curved mustache. Holly was quick to point out that he was working undercover at the moment. That explained the costume he wore.

The waitress returned and asked if she could bring more coffee. Holly said yes, with cream, and Armund ordered a Corona beer. Holly and Dix gave him a curious look.

"It's ten o'clock. I always drink a beer at ten." He smiled and shrugged his shoulders, as if to say *that's what I do*.

"So, Dix," began Holly, "have you really crossed to the other side?"

"What do you mean, Holly?"

"If you remember, when we were working patrol with Sac PD we were known as the "lock-em-ups," and probation officers were known as the "let-em-outs." We were never on the same page."

Dix laughed. "I have matured, as you said. I no longer want to pound my kidneys riding around eight hours in a patrol car. Now I get to ride when I want to in a comfortable car of my choice, and I get to deal with those who have been let out. No more street hassles with drunks."

The waitress returned and took their orders. Scrambled with bacon and wheat toast for Dix. Spanish omelet for Armund, with a large side of salsa, and toast and a fruit bowl for Holly.

"So, what's it been, over six years since we left the PD? How has life been treating you, Holly," asked Dix.

"All that time with the Bureau of narcotic Enforcement, BNE, and much of it undercover work. I have a lot of independence and work my cases as I want, within certain limits. Married one time for about four months. He apparently got bored with me and started dipping his wick in all the strange stuff that would hold still long enough. I told him that if he had another inch or two, he could get some strange stuff at home, then I kicked him hard in the balls and filed for divorce. No permanent relationships since then, and none wanted. And you, Dix, where did life take you?"

Dix offered a summary of his life since he left Sac PD. "I joined the Navy in August 1961 and was assigned to a SEALS team after basic training and SEALS training. Spent most of my time in and around Vietnam, sometimes in the north and sometimes in the south..."

"SEALS," interrupted Hernandez, "Is that some sort of Special Forces?"

"Yes," Dix replied. "They do an array of special ops, like underwater demolition, intelligence, ` guerilla fighting, and sniping."

"Sounds dangerous." Hernandez replied.

"A thrill a minute," Dix retorted. "Although not always positive. Anyway, an accident occurred during an underwater demolition training session in October 1964 that blew out my right eardrum. I was given a choice of a desk or a discharge. I took the discharge and moved back to Riverton and lived with my mother for a few months. She later passed away. The Vet's Hospital staff repaired my eardrum, but kept me on a partially disabled pension. In January 1965 I was hired as an investigator with the local district attorney's office. Did criminal investigations for eight or nine months, but then fell out of favor with my supervisor because of political differences. He was a flaming fascist and I wasn't. Reassigned me to handle their non-support cases, collecting child support from deadbeat fathers. Within a few months that entire work unit was transferred downstairs to the adult division of the probation department. I wouldn't be surprised if he didn't arrange that as well. However, one of the probation officers retired recently, and I was assigned to cover his caseload. The non-support cases were transferred back to the DA."

"I'll bet that broke your heart," commented Holly.

"It did...NOT...said Dix. I have enjoyed my short time supervising the criminal cases, although the confrontations with those two narcs I mentioned has dampened my satisfaction of work."

The waitress returned with their orders. Armund requested more sauce.

"Now that we are updated on each of our life stories, Dix," said Holly, "let's move on to talk about those two narcs. Armund and I have been working together for about nine months tracking down one of the large narcotic distribution networks on the west coast. He was working for CBI, but is now on loan to BNE because he knows so much about the drug operations. I'll let him fill you in."

Armund had eaten half of his omelet already, but he paused to talk to Dix. "The drug distribution network we're tracking runs an operation that ranges from Canada to Mexico, and the I-5 freeway corridor is their primary conduit," explained Hernandez. "Heroin and meth and marijuana flow in from Canada or Mexico and carriers distribute them on a regular route, with many drop-offs going down the I-5. The main carrier drives down 5 and meets a secondary carrier at specific stops along the way south. His first stop in California is Redding. The secondary carrier takes the deliveries for the coastal towns and takes 120 to Ukiah for his first drop. He then drives down 101 to a drop spot just above Cloverdale. Your guys, Bozeman and Simmons meet him there and get their share for distribution around Ramona County. Bozeman and friend control all the sales in your area. Our entire team has a plan to bust all the carriers on next Saturday. That would dry up narcotic sales here for a while, but we would only get them for transportation for sale and sale. It would get them a few years alright, but now with the information you've given Holly about the two murders, maybe we can put your two guys away for life."

Dix described what Fred's probationer had told him about the narc raid at the home in Windsor and the shooting of the probationer's brother and friend, and how they planted throw-away guns, looted the place of cash and drugs, primarily LSD.

"Do you think that the probationer will testify to that in court?"

"Absolutely. I think we will find that a number of guys will be willing to come forward and testify against Bozeman if they think it will bring him down."

"Here's what I'm thinking," offered Holly. "We need a place to trap Bozeman and Simmons; a place where they can't get away, and where we can confront them in a manner that will elicit a confession. We need a straw man to suck them in."

"We have two elements that we can factor into your idea to appeal to Bozeman's greed, his ego, and his hate for me and for one of my probationers," offered Dix.

Dix detailed his run-ins with Bozeman and Simmons and with their run-in with his probationer Morton Shoenfield. He also described the old man Lieutenant Charles Collins and the long drive up to his secluded house. A perfect place to lure Bozeman. He already thinks it's a drug haven.

As Dix explained, "Bozeman will do anything to get at me and Shoenfield."

Hernandez interrupted with an idea. "I see this coming together something like this. For the past two drops made to Bozeman, I have been the driver, and the usual guy, Rico, that has been making the drops for about a year, was with me and handled the drop. He introduced me to Bozeman and Simmons as the man who might be making future drops. Of course, they didn't know that we had already arrested Rico and charged him with transportation. He had a long rap sheet, and we promised him at least ten years in the whizzer unless he cooperated. He was quick to make a deal. He helped me get inside on the drops and we placed him in a witness protection program, with a house, car, and new ID. So now I'll make the drops alone. My next drop with Bozeman is Saturday. I'll tell him that we are splitting the pie from now on because we have a new player on the street. I'll hold back a quarter of what would have been Bozeman's stash, but the price remains the same. He will not like it, but he'll drive back home, going south on 101, and hide, expecting me to come along and then follow me to the new guy."

"Wait a minute," interrupted Dix. If he doesn't like the cut, he is just as likely to shoot you and take it all, along with any other dope and cash you might have. Then he'll blame it on the result of some drug war."

"Okay, so I'll have a car with two other agents with automatic weapons follow me and stop with me when I meet with Bozeman for the drop. My two guys show their weapons and I assure Bozeman that here's the new deal. Take it or leave it. Then I'll drive south and after a few minutes, my guys will turn around and head north, the way we came. He'll never know what happened. Then, the following Friday I'll stop to make the drop to Bozeman, only I'll tell him that he gets the quarter share this time and the rest is going to the new player. I'll have two other guys with me riding shotgun, just in case Bozeman starts thinking about robbing me for the lot. Then I'll drive south on the 101 and allow him to follow me. I drive out to where your guy lives, and we drive up that long driveway and wait for the narcs. You're up there with Holly waiting for Bozeman. He sees you and you openly confront him about the two shootings at the drug house. He thinks he's got the upper hand and tells all. Then we come out and make the arrest.

Dix saw Hernandez as a quick study of the situation who had a very feasible play to offer, but there were several aspects to work out.

"Maybe you could pick me up on the way, in some obvious place, to make it easy for Bozeman to follow," Suggested Dix.

"Sounds like a good idea," Hernandez replied. I'll call you next week in the evening to agree on a place to meet."

"So, you're offering me as a sacrificial goat to face Bozeman."

"No problem for you," replied Hernandez.

"Easy for you to say," joked Dix. "Also, I'll have to get my probationer's cooperation and through him, the cooperation of old man Collins. I'll need to be able to offer them something for their cooperation."

"What did you have in mind?" asked Holly.

"Money, for one thing. It is always an incentive. Can you offer to rent the property from Collins for the time we are there, say $1,000?"

"We can do that," responded Armund. We can even go to $2,000. There is plenty of *by* money in my budget. Make it worth his time. What about your probationer?"

"I can offer to petition the court to terminate his probation and expunge his record. He deserves that anyway."

"Sounds like we have a deal," said Armund.

"I'll need to meet with them soon to work it out. It might be useful if Holly could accompany me to meet with them."

"I could go with you later today," said Holly.

"Sure. Let's do it. I'll follow you back to your motel in Santa Lisa, and we can go from there," replied Dix.

"Okay. That works for me too. I'm staying at the Firebird Motel, the one tucked behind that row of redwood trees near the Pink Flamingo Hotel."

"Firebird Motel! I know where that is. If I lose you in traffic, I'll see you there."

"They split the check and paid, and were about ready to leave, when Dix thought of something. "I am in tight with one of my probationers and I think he will help us out. I could have him drop the hint that there is a new dealer in town who will soon be taking over distribution in the area. We know that one of his group is a snitch and we might be able to plant the seed with Bozeman that I am the one taking over."

"That might help," replied Hernandez, "but be careful how it comes out."

"Not to worry," said Dix.

They said their goodbyes and drove away.

Chapter Twenty-Three

As Dix drove into the Firebird Motel parking area, Holly came out of the lobby and got into his car. Holly must have driven ahead of Dix on the drive home because she had time to change her clothes and freshened up

They drove out of the motel parking lot and straight down Farmers Lane for six blocks, where it ended at Linden Valley Road; they drove east on Linden Valley for about five miles. He made sure along the way that they had not been followed. They turned south on Ramona Mountain Road for a few miles and stopped at the old farmhouse where Dix had first met Shoenfield. Dix parked alongside the house and got out of the car.

"You better wait here until I'm sure Mort is here, and then we'll come out to the car," said Dix.

He walked around to the back of the house and looked toward the hut where he had first seen Shoenfield. No sign of anyone. He called out, "Hey Mort, it's me, Monroe."

Mort came out the back door of the house. "I heard you drive up, but I wasn't sure who is was. Another visit so soon?" he queried.

"In a way, Mort. Only this time we're here to ask your help with a scheme of ours."

"Who do you mean, *we?*"

"I have an associate with me. She is waiting in the car. I'd like you to meet her and listen to our idea for putting Bozeman and Simmons down and out."

"Now that sounds intriguing." Mort walked down the back stairs and followed Dix to the car. Holly got out of the car to greet them.

"Mort, this is Holly Trent. She is a special agent with BNE. Holly, this is Morton Shoenfield."

They shook hands, and Mort looked her up and down, and then gazed back and forth between her and Dix, trying to assess the situation.

"So, what's the skinny?" Mort asked.

"Mort," began Holly, "Dix and I have a plan to trap Bozeman and Simmons and arrest them for at least two murders, burglary, stealing firearms, and transporting and selling drugs and narcotics. This is just part of a state-wide investigation that BNE and CBI have been conducting for over the past year. We are now ready to strike with simultaneous state-wide arrests. We need your help and that of your friend, Mr. Collins, up that hillside drive. We expect to get those two narcs off the street and into prison for a long time."

"Wow!" responded Shoenfield. "Sounds fantastic. However, I have three questions: how will you do that? What is the risk for me? And what's in it for me, and for Collins?"

"Good questions," responded Holly. Our plan goes something like this. The drug distribution network we have been investigating runs drugs between Canada and Mexico, and all points in between, using I-5 as the primary network connecter. One of my associates with BNE has worked his way inside the drug cartel and is now one of the drug couriers who picks up a supply of drugs, mainly heroin and marijuana, at a point on the 5, and delivers them to drops in Mendo and Ramona counties. Bozeman and Simmons are the two who receive all the drugs for Ramona County. They then distribute them to their local sellers. Next Saturday my guy will meet with Bozeman and Simmons for the drop, but will only give them three-fourths of their usual supply. We will tell them that a new player is coming on. We expect them to become angry and to attempt to follow my guy to see who that new player is. However, he will drive away and lose them. The following Wednesday, he will meet with Bozeman and Simmons, but give them only half of their usual supply and we'll tell them that the new player is moving in to take control over some of the territory. This time, we expect Bozeman and Simmons to follow our guy, who will allow himself to be followed and will stop in town and pick up Monroe. They will then drive out to Collins place and set up the ambush for

Bozeman and Simmons, assuming that they have followed our guy. You and Collins will wait inside the house, well protected, and we will confront the two outside and settle the matter."

Mort looked at Dix and Holly for a long minute and then said, "What intrigue. Sounds like a real spy novel. My part is just to help you gain Collins' support and to wait for the outcome?"

"Exactly," said Dix.

"And, my third question again: what do I get out of this, besides being rid of those two assholes?"

"I will prepare a report and submit it to the court requesting the honorable termination of your probation and a reduction of the offense to a misdemeanor and the expungement of your record."

"You can do that?" asked Mort.

"I can and I will. Now I can't guarantee that the judge will honor my request, but I have a solid reputation with the courts and have never had them deny a request of mine."

"Oh man, I can dig that all the way. But why would you do that for me?"

"I forgot; you are the suspicious guy. There are two facets to my job. One is to provide direction so that you will obey the terms of your probation and, the other is to help you where I can. I don't think you need my direction. You're making good decisions on your own, and the best way I can help you is to cut you loose."

"Monroe, you've been straight with me all the way, unlike anyone else I have run into in the justice system, and I'll help all the way with this."

"Will you come with us to visit Collins and finalize our plans?" asked Dix.

"Let's go," responded Mort. He was getting excited at the thought of the scheme and was grinning from ear to ear.

They all got in Dix's car and drove up the hill to Collins' house. The huge oak and madrone trees shrouded the drive so much that it reminded Holly of a tunnel.

Dix parked about thirty yards from the house, and they all got out of the car and stood, waiting for Collins to come out.

Mr. Collins came out the front door, wearing those same bib overalls a red flannel shirt. He had to strain his eyes to identify who was standing there. Finally, he said, "Mort, you young scallywag, and Dix and a pretty lady. Nice to see you all."

Collins walked toward the other three. "To what do I owe the pleasure of your company? And who is that pretty lady you brought to visit?"

Holly stepped forward to meet Collins and said, "I'm not sure that I can pass for a lady, but my name is Holly Trent and we came to ask for your support and cooperation in a scheme we've devised to capture some bad guys."

"I'm Charlie Collins, at your service, Holly. That sounds like a gravid idea, whatever it is. And you might not be a lady, but you certainly are a fine-looking woman."

"Thank you, Charlie. I can tell that you must have been quite a *jack-the-lad* in your day."

"And my day is not yet over." He and Holly laughed with each other.

"Come on inside where it's warm," directed Charlie. "Fill me in on this devilish scheme you're hatching."

Dix knew what to expect inside the house. The house was sheltered by several overhanging oak and madrone trees, and it probably rarely saw direct sunlight. Inside, the living room walls had a faded floral print design. There was an old sofa with a dark brown cover, and there were two overstuffed chairs to match. An old, worn oak coffee table was centered between the sofa and chairs. Charlie had a floor lamp on in the small living room by which they could all see, but even in the daylight it still would not have been enough light by which to read. Off the living room was a small kitchen, where Jimmy went to pour some coffee that he had made earlier. A darkened hallway led off the living room to two bedrooms and a bathroom.

Charlie Collins brought in a tray with mugs, sugar, and cream, and a pot of coffee. "Here you go," he said. "It might be strong, but it's hot and friendly."

He poured mugs full for everyone and offered the cream and sugar. Then he settled into one of the overstuffed chairs and said, "Gentlemen and pretty woman, I'm all ears."

Dix and Holly took turns detailing their plan to lure and arrest Bozeman and Simmons. Jimmy Collins listened without saying a word. When they had finished, he said, "You mean that I'm not going to get the opportunity to shoot one of those bastards?"

"You're right, Charlie. You are not going to get that opportunity. You are going to be inside the house. If anyone does any shooting, it will be us. And there will be plenty of us here to do the job," said Holly.

"Well, at least we can watch from the front window," Collins said. "How many of you will be here?"

"There will be Dix and I and my associate, Armund, outside waiting to greet Bozeman and Simmons. Armund carries a remodeled Winchester Model 1897 trench gun, a five-shot pump 12-gauge, with a 20-inch barrel, effective at close range. He and Dix will be standing out front to greet Bozeman. I will be standing alongside your house, just back in the shadows, with a Winchester Model 70 rifle, with a Swarovichi 1.5 scope. I will pick my shots, if necessary, to stop Bozeman without killing him. We will have two other agents waiting in your house with you, just in case. They will be armed with M16 -5.56 mm NATO automatic rifles. We will also have an ambulance and a tow truck standing nearby if needed. I expect that Bozeman will be following closely behind Armund and Dix, so we will have our other two agents come here first. They will be driving a 2-door 1965 black Chevrolet, and they will have automatic weapons with them."

"Sounds as though you are ready for World War III," commented Mort.

"We want to cover all the contingencies, and we don't want anyone to get hurt. At lease none of us. We also want to take Bozeman alive so he can stand trial. It would be an empty victory if he were to be shot in the process."

"Any questions?" Holly asked.

"What happens if there is damage to my house or property?" Jimmy asked.

"Good point, Charlie. We almost forgot what we planned for you. We want to arrange it so that we rent your property for those few hours and pay you $2,000 in rent and for your time and trouble. Mort, we want to pay you $1,000 for your time and trouble. It will be cash in hand at the close of the day."

Mort and Charlie Collins looked at each other and grinned. Charlie responded, "My house is your house," and Mort said, "That is certainly a fair minimum wage."

"Okay, it's a go. Friday at about one p.m. I and two other agents will be here by noon."

Chapter Twenty-Four

Dix and Holly left Collins' house and drove back to Holly's motel. "What do you think of the setup at the house?" Asked Dix.

"It seems ideal for me. I'll park backed in along the south side of the house. You and Armund can back in on the north side of the lot, but stay about twenty yards from the house. Armund can be waiting near his car, and I'll be in that shadowy area between my car and the house. I'll cover the driver's side of their car as Bozeman drives on the lot. Armund can cover Simmons. You stand sort of in the middle, but be sure you are not between me and Bozeman. It will be up to you to initiate the conversation."

"Should I be armed while I am facing them?"

"You might want to carry a gun, but don't have it drawn when they arrive. We want this to develop into as much conversation as possible to draw them out and have them describe their illegal activities. Don't worry. If either of them goes for their weapon, Armund and I will cover you."

Holly tried to make light of any risk posed for Dix, but he wasn't convinced. He knew that she meant well, but he also knew that Bozeman and Simmons were hot-headed and had only limited control over the aggressive bent of their behavior. He took comfort in the fact that he had faced many more serious situations while in the Navy.

"Dix pulled up to Holly's motel room door. "Keep in touch. Let me know how Armund's drop tomorrow goes, and any changes that will have to make."

"Can I entice you to come in for a drink?"

"It's too early for me, Holly. And besides, I would be afraid that you might try to entice me into something else."

"There was a time, Dix, when you liked it, and I wouldn't have to ask you to come and get it."

"I'm not saying that I wouldn't like it. It's as I said before, I'm committed to someone, and I'm not the kind to stray. You know the saying, 'If you stray, you pay.'"

"You always were true blue, Dix. Even when we were dating way back when, I knew that my roommate was hitting on you every chance she got, but that you always turned her down. I admired that about you then, but now it gets in the way of my wanting you."

"I guess that's the price of fame, Holly. You know that we cannot always get what we want."

"I know, but it never hurts to try. See you, Dix."

Dix drove out of the motel parking lot, waving goodbye to Holly as he did. She returned the wave and blew him a kiss.

Dix decided that it was a good time to locate White Shoes Johnson and plant the information about a new player taking over distribution in the south area. He drove to what Rickter had told him was the heart of the bad-ass territory. He parked his car in a well-lighted area alongside a small market and liquor store in a strip mall near where he'd met White Shoes before.

Dix scanned the strip mall stores. Even at this hour their neon signs flashed their gaudy colors beckoning customers to enter and buy the beer, cigarettes, whisky, donuts, groceries, and a hot meal. A microcosm of the town.

He hadn't parked more than five minutes and was still sitting in his car when he was spotted three young black men wearing dark hoodies came toward him.

They got within ten feet of him when one of the men stopped, flipped back his hoodie, and said "Hey, Mr. Monroe. It's me, Jimmy Johnson, White Shoes. What're y'all doing parked out here?"

"I just thought I would spend some time in your neighborhood, watch the action in the area and maybe meet a few of my probationers, like you. What are you up to?"

"We're just out and about, "Looking for the Heart of Saturday Night."

"It's not Saturday, Jimmy."

"We know. But we be looking for that every day and night."

"Well what's happening today?"

"We just being cool here, staying out of the way of that narc."

"You mean Bozeman?"

"Yeah, man. He usually be looking to score here on Friday nights."

"What do you mean *score*?"

"He comes looking for people to rip off their drugs and money. My friend here, Jonas, got beat up trying to buy some dope from a friend here. A lot of guys get their main supply of drugs now so they be good over the weekend. The narc finds them and takes their stuff, promising not to bust them if they say where they got the dope. Then he busts that seller, takes their money and dope and beats the shit out of them and tells them to leave town or get dead, unless it is one of his sellers."

"What do you mean, *one of his sellers*?"

"He tries to control the drug sales in the area. He has a big supplier somewhere that he gets his dope from and he runs a few dealers on the street that supplies us. He stomps on the completion, man, and there is nothing any of us can do. He's the man. He got the badge and gun and there ain't no one going to face him on it."

"Can you prove any of this?"

"No. He keeps clean on the outside, but inside he's a dirtbag. There ain't no one to complain to, because he's the narc in charge around here."

"What if I got together with some of your guys and us a come up with a way to get around Bozeman?"

"Well, Mr. Monroe, that might something to think about, but you see, we're not sure who you are or what your intentions are. We got to get to know you better before we're willing to talk openly with you."

Dix hadn't considered that. Hadn't considered that he might not be trusted, or that they might think he had some hidden agenda.

That exposes that continuing problem a probation officer faces in relating to his clients. He's the authority figure they have to relate to. He's the man with the badge and handcuffs who is saying, "I'm here to help you, but if you screw up, I'm here to bust you." That always works against having the clients trust the PO. It would take time.

"What if you all got together to outsmart him. Keep the dope hidden and keep off the streets?"

"My buddy, Lamar, had a plan once," replied Jimmy. "He got a few of the guys together at his house one night to organize. Bozeman learned about it, came busting in and shot Lamar and two other guys in the bust. Everyone else split, man. The detectives were called in and found evidence of drugs and guns. The shootings were in self-defense because two of the guns had been fired and a few of the slugs were found in the wall around the doorway. One gun was untraceable, and the other was traced to a robbery that happened a year ago in which the in which the robbers were caught and their guns confiscated and held as evidence. Now, no one knew where they came from, and Bozeman and his fat little pal skated. They always do."

"That sounds as though there is a rat in the group. Someone tipped Bozeman. Now who can you trust?"

"That's the problem. We don't know. We gotta' be cool, else we gonna' get popped when we're not looking."

"Jimmy, I came out here looking for you. I need your help with a problem we both have. Is think I can trust you."

"Oh, well then, what 'cha need? You can trust me."

"You know how you and all your friends, and me as well, have been having troubles with those narcs, Bozeman and Simmons?"

"Yea."

"Well, I and some friends of mine have come up with a way to end all those troubles. To stop Bozeman and Simmons. We learned that they are the major distributors of drugs in the county. They have been able to control it so far by either killing or intimidating the competition, including your friend and those two guys in Windsor the other night. We have learned who the source of their drugs is, and we are going to control what they can buy. I want you to casually leak the word that you know that there is a new drug supplier coming to the area and that soon people will be able to buy what they need at a better price and without getting hurt. Can you do that?"

"Is that true, Mr. Monroe. You gonna' take over his territory?"

"No, it's not true, Jimmy. We are actually going to put them out of business, but not replace them ourselves. We just want to get them out and put them in jail for all the dirt they've done. Can you help me, Jimmy?"

"I'm glad to hear that. I figured you for one of the good guys, and I don't want to be disappointed."

"Well, thanks, Jimmy. You just let the word leak out and we'll take it from there. And Jimmy, I'm trusting you, like you trust me. If all goes well, you will have the narcs off your back. No more worries.

"You would do that for me?"

"Yes, I will, Jimmy. Is it a deal?"

"It's a deal," replied Jimmy. This is gonna be a sweet deal. I'm gonna' enjoy watching this go down."

Jimmy moved away from Dix's car and wandered to the other end of the strip mall, grinning all the way.

Dix drove back to the probation department. It was after five p.m. and Fred Connors and Jim Short were the only deputies in the office. Dix greeted each of them and went to his desk. He pulled a few files, including Shoenfield's and Jimmy White Shoes', and took them back to the coffee room. On the way he nodded to Fred to follow him.

Dix sat down at the far end of the long table, farthest away from the door, and sat down. Fred walked in, poured himself a cup of coffee, and joined Dix.

"Did you want to talk, Dix?" Fred asked.

"I do," Dix replied. "Have you had any more contact with your probationer who saw that shooting at the drug house?"

"I talked with him this morning. Told him that you and I were working on a plan to make that right. Have you come up with something?"

"I have Fred, but this is really secret. I can't even tell you the details. And I need your word not to talk any more about it."

"Dix, you have my word and my undying gratitude if this takes those narcs out of the game."

"I knew that I could count on you. I have several state DOJ agents involved, and we have a strategy that will go down on Friday. Bozeman and Simmons will be arrested be for transportation and sales of drugs and narcotics, theft of firearms, and at least two homicides. That is where your probationer comes in. At some point, he will be asked to testify to what he saw. He will get all the protection he needs. We might even be able to hide his identity through most of the proceedings. However, don't say anything to him until my deal is complete. I'll let you know. We can't take a chance that anything will leak before then."

"Just keep me in the loop and we'll be ready. Are you putting yourself at risk in any of this?"

"Maybe just a little, but I should be well covered."

Dix knew that what he was saying might just be wishful thinking. He knew that arresting Bozeman and Simmons wouldn't come easy. There will undoubtedly be some shooting, and those two will blame him for their situation and that he will be the first one in their sights. He also didn't know if Armund Hernandez was a cowboy or if he could keep a cool head. He trusted Holly to control the day. He also hoped that they would take Bozeman and Simmons alive, because he wanted them to face the entire criminal justice process from the criminal's side of the play and get every year in prison that they deserved.

Fred rose from the table and picked up his cup. "Thanks, Dix. I look forward to the end of those two weasels."

Dix left the office and drove to the gym on Fourth Street. He didn't go there for a workout this time, he just wanted to buy a pair of speedbag gloves, a medium size that he thought would fit Billy. He wanted to take them to give to Billy that night.

Dix drove straight to Ultumia However, going straight there from Santa Rosa meant taking a series of backroads, and it took forty-five minutes to get there.

He came in the north end of town and passed the hardware store before arriving at the inn. He noticed that there was a realtor's "For Sale" signs hanging on posts in front of the hardware store and the house next door. Morgan was serious about selling. Dix pulled up and parked in front of the store and went in. Morgan was just finishing up waiting on a customer.

As the customer was leaving, Morgan said, "Evening Dix."

"Evening Trace," replied Dix. "I see by the signs that you are serious about selling. Anything happen to push up your desire to leave?"

"Nothing really happened, except that my wife says that she is moving into a retirement community. You know, one of those where all your meals are prepared and all your other needs are met. She wants to make some friends and get involved with people activities."

"That doesn't sound like your kind of retirement."

"It's not, but if I want to keep living with my wife, that the way it's going to be. I'll work out something to keep my privacy, yet stay active."

"Okay, so if I was really serious about buying your store, should I talk to you or to the realtor?"

"The realtor. It is all in her hands now, and you can buy the store with or without the house."

"How much for just the store?"

"$85,000 for the store, including the property, building, and all the inventory."

"Is the inventory clearly owned by you?"

"Absolutely. All bought and paid for. However, there is a first deed of trust owing on the property of $34,000. Payable to Bank of America in Valley Ford at $100 a month. I don't know if that is assumable or if you'd have to take out a new loan."

"And how soon after the sale would be leaving?"

"The day escrow closes, I'm out of here. And I won't be having any special closeout sale of merchandise in the meantime, if that's a concern to you."

"Okay, Trace. Thanks for the information."

"Are you ready to buy, Dix?"

"No. I'm still in the mulling stage. I took down the name of the realtor incase just in case."

"I was wondering, Dix, why you asked only about the store and not about the house. It's a nice three-bedroom place. A little old, but....now I get it." And Trace stopped his comments.

"What do you get, Trace?"

He looked down toward the direction of the inn. "Should I spell it out for you?"

Dix understood Trace's meaning. If he and Cluny married, they would use her house, which is larger and nicer, and he wouldn't need Trace's house.

"No. There is no need. You're a sly old fox." Traced grinned, "But let me ask you a favor: don't spread the word that I am interested. I'm thinking now that a hardware store is the last thing that I need."

"Sometimes, Dix, the last thing we need is the best for us. I think it would be best for you."

"You might be right, Trace. It's getting complicated for me now."

Dix and Trace said their goodbyes, and Dix drove down to the inn and parked. He assumed that Cluny would be there working by this hour.

Cluny was just walking out of the dining room to the inn lobby as Dix entered. She was surprised to see him, but immediately came to him. They hugged and kissed.

"You didn't call, and I didn't know if I would see you tonight. This is a nice surprise."

"I know that this is your busy time, so I won't stay long. I just wanted to see you."

"I'm so glad you did. I wish we had more time and the place to be intimate. I'm wanting you all the time now, Dix. See what you started."

"Me? You're the one who started it all, and I am ever so glad. Maybe we could step back into your office for just a few minutes?"

"Sorry, Dix. Billy is back there and I have to get to work."

"What about tomorrow. Can we have some time together tomorrow?"

"I thought that you, Billy, and I could take a nice drive; a drive that very few have the access to take it."

"Wow, you sound so mysterious."

"I have a friend who owns a large ranch near Olema. His property runs from near the town all the way to the ocean. We can take his private road and have a beach all to ourselves. We can stop on the way and pick up some sandwiches and stuff to take for a picnic."

"It does sound nice, but I will have to be back by 4:00 p.m."

"It's a date, then. I pick you two up about nine a.m."

"I look forward to it."

"Before I go, I have something to give to Billy."

Dix took a small wrapped package from his jacket pocket. "Here, Billy. I thought you might need these."

Billy tore off the paper and found the small gloves. He wasn't sure what they were for, and he gave Dix a questioning look.

"Those are speedbag gloves, Billy. They keep your knuckles from getting all skinned up when you practice your speed bag."

"Wow, Dix. For me?"

"We can't have you hurting yourself while I teach you how to use the bag, now can we."

"No, sir, we can't. Thank you, Dix. That's super."

"Billy, you better go back to the room while I finish serving my dinner guests."

"Bye Dix. See you tomorrow."

"You got it Billy."

"That was nice of you, Dix. He's thrilled. I think he likes you."

"He's a wonderful boy, Cluny. We're going to enjoy each other."

Chapter Twenty-Five

Dix rose at about seven a.m. He set the coffee to brew and then shaved and showered. Toast and coffee were enough for breakfast. He planned to enjoy their picnic lunch. He put his wallet, binoculars, and his Beretta .380 in a fanny pack and was on his way out the door a little after eight.

There was very little traffic in town. A few merchants and their employees scurrying to find an all-day parking somewhere near their businesses.

The usual morning fog was thinning out in town, but was still heavy on the road to Ultumia. However, by the time he reached Cluny's house, it had all but disappeared. There was no wind up, and a warm day was predicted.

He arrived at Cluny's house just before nine. He found Cluny and Billy, waiting on the porch. Billy with an excited grin, and Cluny with a warm smile and then a kiss.

They drove south on Coast Highway 1 for about seventeen miles, along the east shore of Tomales Bay, and down into Point Reyes Station, a small village a few miles south of the Bay. The downtown area was one long block, with a Standard service station, three taverns, a grocery store, Chevy dealership, a deli, and a combination lumber/hardware store. It obviously was not a destination spot, but provided for most of the needs of the villagers and surrounding farmers.

Dix stopped at Stormy's Deli at the end of the street. They went inside to buy food for their picnic. Dix and Cluny ordered pastrami and Swiss cheese on sourdough rolls, with all the extras, and Billy ordered peanut butter and jelly on white bread. Not an adventurer. They bought chips and sodas, as well, and placed everything in a wicker basket Cluny brought with her.

They drove a quarter-mile south out of town and turned righted right on Francis Drake Boulevard as it intersected with Highway 1. That road led to the village of Inverness, and then on to Drake's Bay and the Point Reyes Lighthouse. However, after about one mile they turned south on Bear Valley Road, a four-mile backroad that connects to Highway 1 again at Olema, a wide spot in the road called a village.

Two miles down Bear Valley Road they came to the entrance to Bear Valley Ranch, identified by an elaborate heavy wooden gate and archway with the name spelled out in small cuts of timber.

Dix drove in and stopped at the gate; they were immediately met by the owner, Richard "Buck" Coulter, a man of about seventy, five-feet-seven-inches tall and four feet around at the waist. He wore Levi's, a western style shirt, tall Stetson hat, and a huge oval belt buckle that featured an engraved cowboy on horseback, roping a bull.

Buck opened the gate and Dix drove in and stopped.

He got out of the car. Buck greeted him with a warm handshake and a big, awkward bear hug. Dix brought Buck to the car and introduced him to Cluny and Billy.

"Well I'm mighty pleased to meet you Cluny, and Billy. My ranch is at your disposal, and I'm sure that you will enjoy the day."

Buck pointed to his jeep parked just off the road by the arena and said, "Take my jeep, Dix. It will be more fun riding in an open car, and you won't have to worry about getting stuck anywhere. I'm down here doing some minor repairs on the arena. I'll take your car back to the house and meet you folks there later."

Cluny stepped out of the car and came around the front and shook Buck's hand. "Thank you for the hospitality. What's the arena for?"

"That's for our annual rodeo, Cluny. Fourth of July every year, folks from around the area meet here and we have a big-time rodeo and barbecue. Some folks come over from the valley as well. We have calf roping, bull riding, bull-dogging, and bucking horse riding. It's great fun. Did Dix tell you about his attempt at bull dogging on the Fourth?"

"No, he didn't," replied Cluny. "Tell me about it."

"No, Buck," interjected Dix. I think we should go. We're in a hurry."

"We're not in that much of a hurry," said Cluny.

"Do you know what bull-dogging is, Cluny?" asked Buck.

"Isn't that where the rider guides his horse alongside a running bull and then leaps from the saddle and grabs the bull by the horns and turns him to the ground?"

"Exactly," Buck confirmed. "Only Dix forgot the most important step in the process. He was supposed to lean from the horse and grab a horn with one hand and then let the horse carry his feet past the steer until his feet naturally fall out of the stirrups. That way his legs are in front of him, and he can dig in with his heels. Then he has the leverage to twist the head of the steer and finally cause the steer to become unbalanced and fall to the ground. Dix slid off the horse and didn't let his legs get in front of him, so he had no leverage and the bull dragged him for twenty yards before Dix had to let go."

Buck was laughing so hard at his own description that it was difficult for him to finish the tale. Cluny joined right in with the laughter, trying to imagine the sight that Buck was trying to describe.

"Real funny, Buck," said Dix. I knew that I shouldn't have introduced you to Cluny. You've probably been dying to tell that story ever since you knew we were coming out here." Then Dix joined in the laughter and admitted that he had a lot to learn about bulldogging.

"Next time, Buck. I'll come out and take of couple of lessons before the rodeo, and then I'll show you who the better bulldogger is."

"There might not be a next time, Dix. The Feds are moving to take all this property along the coast for a national park. It will become the Point Reyes National Seashore if they have their way. Congress authorized a bill to create it, and it was signed into legislation by President John Kennedy on September 13, 1962. It includes approximately 70,000 acres and twenty-seven working cattle and dairy ranches. Word quickly got out that the Feds were offering to buy the land, so the prices rose dramatically and the Feds' budget for the project emptied quickly."

"That must have stirred up a lot of controversy from those who didn't want to sell."

"It sure did, and that hasn't settled down yet. You know at the turn of the century there were some forty dairy ranches in the area. Many of them were formed from parts of original Mexican land grants. Most of the immigrants who settled on these ranches were primarily Swiss-Italian,

Swedish, and Portuguese. Ranching has been a way of life for several generations of these families. They don't want to lose it. It has irritated some that they will either have to sell or go on some sort of land use, but not ownership, especially when the large religious organization, the Vedanta Society, located just south of my ranch were included in the original park area, but somehow it got an exclusion and will continue to exist independently."

"So how long do you have?"

"Well, it will be by 1972 at the latest. They'll close off all motorized access to this entire area and open it up only to hikers. And maybe later, they will allow horses. Glenda and I will probably have to sell out to them and move. I don't see any other way. We might be able to stay in the house for our lifetimes, but we won't have any control over the land. No more rodeos, my friend. And this might be your last motor ride on our road to the ocean, so enjoy it all now while you can."

"Buck? Isn't there anything you can do?"

"I'm afraid not. It might come this year, or maybe next, but it's coming. You can't stop the Feds once they make their move."

"I'm sorry, Buck. I had no idea. I guess we'll just do as you say for now and enjoy the day. We'll stop back at the house on the way out. Anyone else out there?"

"Yes, our oldest son Alfred and his wife and son. You'll probably find them at the beach."

"Good, I look forward to seeing him again. Say, how's Don?"

Buck looked at Cluny before he answered Dix, and then said "Don's our youngest son."

Then Buck answered Dix, "He's back in Philadelphia, married, you know. That's where Ellen, his wife, is from. She works for some law firm and he works for some nonprofit, counseling vets returning from combat zones. Loves his work."

"That should be right up his alley, and satisfying as well. Tell him I said Hi next time you make contact. We best be on our way. We'll stop at the house on our way back and say hello to Glenda and trade cars."

Dix drove his car over to where the jeep was parked next to Buck's arena and placed their picnic basket and blanket on the floor of the jeep, and then he drove the jeep back for Cluny.

When Dix drove off, Buck looked at Cluny and said, "I just thought you ought to know that you have a good man there, a fine man."

"I know, Buck, and I appreciate you telling me. And just so you know, I'll do right by him."

Dix, Cluny, and Billy waved to Buck and started off down the road, past Buck's ranch house and outbuildings and then on to the ocean. The ride was about six miles along what was known as the Bear Valley Trail. Although it was called a trail, it was plenty wide enough for a vehicle.

"That Buck seems like a real character," said Cluny. "What a shame all this will change for him."

"He sure is that," replied Dix. He is an old rodeo cowboy who never grew up, although he grew rich. He was at one time the national bulldog and calf roping champion of the U.S. Now, every year, he tries to recreate those special moments in his own arena by encouraging an array of young riders to compete. He's a great guy and a good friend. And it is a real shame to see him lose all this. It will be the end of his last dream."

The road cut through a pasture for about a half-mile and then entered a wooded area, thick with coastal Douglas fir, California live oak, and bay trees. A small stream, Bear Valley Creek, ran alongside of the road. Both sides of the road were flanked by lush ferns and other native plants. Farther down the road they saw California poppies, checker bloom, cousin to the hollyhock, with its pink to red-purple flowers and prominent white veins, along with Douglas Iris, a pale lavender in color.

A dirt road made a T-intersection with the trail road just as the pasture ended. Twenty yards up that road was a gate, and just before the gate was a garage or small barn. A walking trail went from the barn, across the creek from the road, but paralleling it for about thirty yards to a flat area on which was built a two-story summer house, painted a dull yellow and trimmed in faded off-white. The house seemed to be planted there between the hillside covered with ferns and bay trees, and the stream. The color scheme actually blended into the surrounding trees and brush.

"Look at that house, Dix. Do you think someone lives there?"

"Not permanently. It is a vacation house that belongs to some wealthy family from Riverton. They draw their water from the stream and use lanterns for lighting because there is no electricity. I've been inside once. It has a large living room with a stone fireplace, a kitchen with a wood stove, and four small bedrooms, all sharing one bathroom. There is a nice deck off the living room that overlooks the creek, as you can see."

"Yes, I see it. It looks dark and cold there."

They drove around a bend in the road and saw a meadow on their left, where another house had been built next to a huge dogwood tree that had large white flowers, the kind that might last until winter.

"That's a house that belongs to some wealthy family from Marin County, but it's rather dark and drab looking. I've never seen anyone there."

"I wonder if these families will have to sell to the Feds and move if this area becomes part of the park?"

"I imagine they will, although there is a religious sect on the adjoining property called the Vedanta Society, and Buck once told me that they were hoping to buy both houses. He didn't know what they planned to do with them," Dix replied.

The road began a slight ascent, but still paralleled the creek for about another mile until it leveled off at the start of a large meadow. The creek that had been running down the incline and past the houses had disappeared somewhere up in the hill above the meadow.

"Look," exclaimed Billy. And he pointed left to where the meadow ended and the tree line began. "What is that moving?"

Dix stopped the jeep and they sat and watched. Dix got out his binoculars to get a better look.

"It is a mountain lion, Billy. This must be his hunting grounds and we've disturbed him." The animal disappeared among the trees.

"Was that a real lion, Dix?" asked Billy.

"No, Billy. It is just a big wild cat that lives in isolated area like this. We'll stay away from him and he will keep away from us. He is scared of people."

Cluny moved a little closer to Dix and put her arm around his shoulder.

"Not to worry," said Dix.

The road was well worn and a little rough in spots, as it began a slight descent toward the ocean. Now they were paralleling another creek that flowed toward the ocean. It must a different creek coming out of the hills above the meadow.

The jeep purred along with no difficulty and was the perfect vehicle from which to enjoy the scenery. Along the way they passed several clearings in which small herds of deer grazed and blue lupines bloomed. They were more in the open now, away from the fern-lined stream. Soon the ocean came into view and Cluny and Billy were excited.

They reached the end of the road and parked next to a Buick convertible, which Dix assumed belonged to Buck's son, Alfred, and his family. Dix took the picnic basket and Cluny carried a blanket. Billy brought along a gunny sack because Dix had said they would find some interesting objects to collect.

The trail to the beach from the parking area was only about twenty feet and not steep. The beach was wide but not deep. Only about thirty yards to the water. They found a comfortable, level place on the sand to spread out the blanket next to a large weathered log that looked as though it had been there for years, and they settled down. Dix could see Alfred and his family sitting about halfway down the beach. Alfred had seen them and was waiving. Dix waived back. He saw that Alfred was walking toward them, and that a young boy was with him, undoubtedly his son.

Alfred was wearing shorts and a light open-neck shirt. He was much taller than his father, and had a lean figure and a big mop of black hair.

Dix rose to meet him. "Alfred, great to see you. Your dad told us that you would be here."

Cluny and Billy both rose, "Alfred, this is Cluny and her son Billy.
"

Cluny, Billy, and Alfred exchanged greetings, and Alfred introduced his son, Jim. He was about Billy's age.

Billy and Jim seemed to warm up to each other, and each seemed glad that someone his own age was here.

"Want to help me look for glass fishing floats along the shore?" Jim asked of Billy.

"Sure. Mom, is it okay?"

"Absolutely," replied Cluny.

"And Billy, stay out of the water and off the cliffs." said Dix,

"Okay, Dix. We will."

"We're going to eat soon, so come back any time you get hungry."

"I'm giving them the ten-dollar tour today and enjoying your family's hospitality," Dix said to Alfred.

"Take it all in, Dix. No one deserves to come here more than you do."

"Thanks, Alfred. We'll come over and see you later."

"He seems like a nice man, Dix, and he certainly doesn't share his father's build."

"No, neither of their sons do. The mother is taller and better looking." They laughed at the comparison.

"What are those glass floats that Jim asked Billy to help him find?"

"They are round, thick glass balls, from four to six inches in diameter, and they have a small glass cap melted over what would have been the hole left after the glass was blown. They are tied onto fishing nets by Japanese fisherman. Occasionally they break away from the net and eventually wash up on our beaches."

"They float all the way across the ocean from Japan?" Cluny asked with a look that indicated either she thought it was amazing or that Dix was kidding.

"They do, Cluny. No one knows how long it takes, but they do float here from Japan. I have a few in my house and yard that I've found over the few years I've come here."

Dix and Cluny sat on the blanket and leaned against the log. She gazed at the ocean the sights around her, thankful that she had brought dark glasses because there was a glare off the water. Dix laid his head on her shoulder and soon was kissing her neck and nibbling her ear.

"Are you hinting at what I think you're hinting at, Dix Monroe?"

"That's what I'm hinting at, Cluny Ramm."

They kissed and then moved down to lie on the blanket and pulled another blanket over them, keeping one eye down the beach in case anyone came toward them. They quickly engaged in what might not have been called making love, but it certainly was great sex.

Afterwards, Dix lay across the blanket and rested his head in Cluny's lap. He smiled and sighed, and felt at peace with the world.

"Dix?"

"Yes?"

"What did Alfred mean earlier when he said that no one deserved to come here and enjoy the site more than you?"

Dix paused and was thinking whether he wanted to talk about that. "It's a long story, Cluny. Maybe when we have more time."

Chapter Twenty-Six

"Out here time doesn't seem to matter and anyway, I have plenty of it," responded Cluny.

"Okay, but don't say that you haven't been warned. It goes back to early in 1963, when I was serving in the navy's SEAL unit. We were assigned to a CIA program named Operation Phoenix that targeted key North Vietnamese Army personnel and Vietcong sympathizers for capture or assassination." Dix recounted the mission as if he were actually re-living it.

Five of us took a Zodiac rubber reconnaissance craft into a small cove near the border between North and South Vietnam. During the next three hours, I led my team of five SEALS around the outskirts of several North Vietnamese villages looking for Viet Cong strongholds. The first four villages we observed were deserted. The locals were either driven out or killed by the Cong. The fifth village appeared deserted initially, but as they lay among the brush that fronted the village, they heard noises in one of the huts. Then a young Vietnamese woman walked out the door with a small child in tow and walked toward them, as if she knew they were there. My orders had been, 'Don'tt shoot unless I give the signal." We watched the girl to determine if she was alone and where she was going, Suddenly, Markley raised his sniper rifle, aimed, and fired before I could react. The young girl fell dead in the street, pulling the child down as she fell. The child got up and started crying, and Markley fired again killing the child. I was shocked and sickened at what Markley had done. I grabbed Markley by the collar and placed my .45 pistol under his chin and said, "You knew my orders not to shoot. Why did you shoot? Why did you have to kill that girl and that child?"

I wanted to pull the trigger and blow his face off, but one of my team members took my arm and pulled it away. He said "He's not worth it, Lieutenant. He's not worth it." That sparked some inner control, and I pulled my finger off the trigger and laid it alongside the trigger guard.

Then I vomited. How could he kill that girl and child without any hesitation or care?

"Well Lieutenant," said Markley, "she was just another geek to me. She was probably walking toward us with a bomb under her skirt. She was the enemy and I took her out."

The men looked back at the village. No sign that anyone else was there and no one responded to the shots fired.

I ordered the men back to the boat and on the way back, that young SEAL who stopped me from killing Markley told Markley that he was nothing but an animal and deserved to be shot like a mad dog. Markley took out his long blade and drew it back to stab the man; I hit Markley as hard as I could on the left side of his face and head with the butt of my rifle. He dropped his knife, yelled, and turned toward me. I hit him again. This time he was out cold. We made it back to the base near Incheon. I immediately made a written and oral reports on Markley's actions to my commander and requested Markley's arrest and court martial.

"Sometimes, when I close my eyes, I can see that woman. He shoots her and she falls dead and her little girl is crying. Then he shoots the little girl. Why did he have to shoot them? How could he shoot..."

Dix turned and buried his face in Cluny's lap and began to sob uncontrollably. He cried for a minute or two. Cluny held him close and stroked his cheek, and then she too was crying.

After a minute or two, Dix turned his head back, and then he sat up and pulled Cluny to him and hugged and held on.

"I've never cried about that incident before. I guess it was there all the time and I finally had to let it out. It felt good. I somehow feel purged,"

"I'm so glad that you did; that you shared that with me. I feel so close to you."

"Hey, are you guys crying or something?" asked Billy. He had returned without them being aware and was standing in the sand next to them.

They both looked up at Billy, and then they began to laugh at the situation.

"Yes, Billy. We were both crying," said Dix. "I told a story and it got sad and we cried. The ending is happy now, so we're laughing."

"Mom told me it was all right for a boy to cry."

"Your mom was right. She is a wise mom. It is all right for anyone to cry if that is how they feel at the moment. Never deny your feelings, Billy. Enjoy them all."

Cluny noticed that Billy was carrying the gunny sack full of something. "What's is in the sack?"

Billy placed the sack down on the blanket and opened it up. It held seven round glass fishing net floats, just like Dix had described.

"Wow. You found some real treasures, Billy," said Dix. "They will be rare before long because these beaches will be opened up to all the public who want to hike out here, and we might not ever be able to drive out here like this again. Save those, Billy. They'll make a nice memory."

Billy told them about all the places they had looked to find the floats and about the tide pools they found; he showed them a handful of what looked like dollar shells. "We found starfish too, but Jim said his dad told him to let them stay in the water. That was their home."

"Those are called sand dollars. They are actually burrowing sea urchins that get washed up on the beach and get bleached by the sun. They look like large silver dollars and each one has a design on it that resembles a picture or symbol that we see in other places in life. Aren't those neat?"

"I'm going to keep these. Say, I'm hungry. Have you guys eaten yet?"

"Not yet, Billy. We were just going to dig in. You're just in time."

Dix and Cluny sat on the blanket and leaned back on the log, and Billy nestled between them, moving them aside until he had room to fit. Cluny opened the picnic basket, and they ate their sandwiches and some chips, and drank their sodas, talking about all the wonders they had seen and could see out at Bear Valley.

After a while, Cluny noticed the time. She had to be back at the inn by three and it was already one-thirty. She pointed to her watch and nudged Dix to look.

"Billy, go say goodbye to Jim and meet us back at the car. We have to go or your mom will be late."

Billy took off running down the beach toward his new friend. Dix and Cluny gathered up the picnic basket and the blanket and headed for the jeep.

On the way Cluny said, "You never did finish telling me what Alfred meant about you having the right to be here."

"Do you recall that man on my team that pulled my arm down when I wanted to shoot Markley and who I later saved when Markley was going to stab him?"

"Yes."

"His name is Don Coulter, Buck's youngest son. He and I were both transferred to a training duty station in South Vietnam. We were friends from then on. He was later discharged, and he looked me up after he returned home. We met out here and I became a friend of Buck's for life."

"That's a nice ending to your story. A small-world story. Thanks again for sharing. By the way, whatever happened to Markley?"

"I heard that he received a dishonorable discharge later that year and was sent back to the U.S. after he shot two more friendly Vietnamese women. Then about a year ago, he climbed the bell tower on a college campus in Philadelphia and began shooting any students within range. Fortunately, someone had the good sense to start the bells ringing. That disoriented him long enough for the police to arrive and take him out."

Cluny was stunned and just stared at Dix for a long minute. Dix waved to Alfred as they left the beach area.

"The problem is, Cluny, they train men for war and to kill, and when they are no longer useful, they dump them back home without any preparation for living among regular people in normal times. Some can't handle the stress and either break or start leading dysfunctional lives. Those are the guys that Don Coulter counsels on his job."

"That's good to hear. They need more of his kind," stated Cluny.

The ride back was just as full of the beauties of nature as it was on the drive out, except that they didn't see any big cats. As they passed the big yellow house across the creek near the beginning of the trail road, they saw two young couples sitting on deck chairs, and three young boys playing in the creek below. Everyone exchanged waves.

"I'll bet that it's quiet out here at night," said Cluny.

"It would be, but during the first few nights one would have to get used to all the night sounds from the animals around here."

They were approaching Buck's house, a large log cabin-style ranch house built on a slope just below the tree line. It had a full deck in front and around both sides. Buck and his wife, Glenda, heard them coming and came out on the front deck to meet them.

"Come on up. Glenda has some fresh lemonade ready."

Dix drove the jeep close to the deck and said, "Hi Glenda." This is Cluny and her son, Billy." They waved and said hi. "We lost track of time and Cluny has to get back. Thanks so much, you two. We had a great day. I'll give you a call and maybe we can do it again before the Feds step in."

"Any time, Dix," replied Buck, "but it had better be soon."

Dix, Cluny, and Billy took their belongings out of the jeep and put them into Dix's car. Cluny stood outside the car for a long moment and gave a final look at Bear Valley.

They drove back to Ultumia, and Dix dropped Cluny and Billy off at Cluny's house.

"See you tomorrow, Billy, said Dix. "Take care of all that loot you found today."

"See ya' Dix," replied Billy as he took his gunny sack and went into his back yard.

"I don't like saying goodbye, but I know that I'll see you tomorrow for dinner," said Dix.

"I feel the same," replied Cluny. "I wish you didn't have to go. You drive safely going home."

They kissed. One of their long kisses. Then Cluny went into the house to dress for work. Dix drove home slowly, reflecting on their day. It felt so natural being with Cluny and Billy. He continued to wonder where this relationship was taking him.

When Dix got home and walked into his living room, he saw the light blinking on his phone answering machine. It was a new type of machine called an *Ansafone,* sold by a company called Phonetel. This company began selling answering machines in 1960, but this one was new to Dix. In fact, this was the first time that anyone had left a message for him.

Dix pushed the play button and heard, "Hi Dix, this is Holly. Everything is going as planned. We'll wait now for the *coup de grâce* on Friday. Call if you have questions."

Chapter Twenty-Seven

Thursday was a strange day. Dix was up early. He put on his running shorts, shoes, and a tee-shirt, and drove up to the high school and parked in back next to the gate allowing entry to the track. There were six or seven others out on the track, running. The usual morning overcast kept the weather cool for the runners.

Dix did the usual morning run: one lap around the football field at a trot, and then he increased his speed with each subsequent lap until he was at a full gait on the sixth and seventh laps. On the last lap he slowed down gradually, and then stretched out on the football field lawn until he could breathe again. Then he went home.

Dix decided not to go to his office in the morning. He called Naomi at the department's front counter to say that he would not be coming into the office until late in the afternoon, if at all. He would be contacting probationers that lived within the Riverton area. They were to be courtesy calls, just to meet them. Nothing more. He had twenty-seven that he had not yet contact, either in person or by phone, and he needed to meet them and inform them of the change in their supervising probation officer.

By one p.m., he had seen nine probationers and left business cards at the homes of the others. Then he drove to three of the small police departments within the county and collected the lists of those firearms that each agency had sent to be destroyed, during the past two years. Hopefully, some of these had serial numbers that would match guns either turned in to the sheriff's department as evidence by Bozeman or Simmons, or would be found in their possession.

Dix was home by four p.m. He was feeling unsettled, caught between not having seen Cluny today and thinking ahead to the scenario that was planned with Bozeman and Simmons.

He called Cluny, hoping to arrange a time that they could be together in the evening. She was full of apologies and explained that she had to cater a fiftieth wedding anniversary dinner that evening for one of the town's noted citizens. She had set it on her calendar several weeks ago, but had forgotten about it during the recent situation with her father and her developing relationship with Dix.

Cluny said that she would make it a point to be completely free Friday and would have her evening staff handle whatever business they had. She and Dix arranged to spend the evening together at his house. She would have Billy spend the evening next door with her parents. If all went well, she would spend the night with Dix as well. That gave them something to look forward to.

Dix wandered around the house for thirty minutes or so like a lost soul. He was looking for something to do, but he couldn't find it, whatever it was. Finally, he got in his car and drove to Mary's Café for dinner.

He ordered the hot beef sandwich and coffee, watching Mary as she moved about behind the counter while he waited for his order. After a few minutes he noticed that Duncan was giving him the evil-eye for looking at Mary for so long. Actually, he was just staring off into space and Mary happened to walk into that space. Nevertheless, he quickly began a conversation with several of the regular patrons. They exchanged pastimes and pleasantries, typical of men having nothing more to do in life, each pausing between bites to allow the others to have their say.

In the middle of all their meaningless exchanges, Dix realized that some of these men are here every night, passing the time just like this every night. *Please spare me,* mused Dix.

Finally, Dix went home. He still didn't feel sleepy so he turned on the television and watched a show he liked on NBC, *The Saint*, staring Roger Moore as Simon Templar, an investigator or perhaps an espionage agent. The story began in Rome, with Simon chatting up some blond on the steps leading to the Coliseum. They were next seen driving off in Templar's sleek sports car, the white Volvo P1800.

Dix suddenly jerked upright and awake when the station played the national anthem. It was midnight, and the network was signing off for the night.

He washed, brushed his teeth, put his clothes away, and got into bed, hoping to sleep through the night. It was not to be. He tossed and turned for a while, and finally sat up, turned on the lamp on the nightstand and began reading a book that had been on the nightstand for months, The *Naked Ape*, by Desmond Morris, a zoologist and ethologist. It was one of the current, popular must-read books. Morris was presenting his view on the evolution of man. There were many sexual references and innuendos as to the purposes of the female body parts that Dix found amusing. No wonder it was popular. Sex sells.

It wasn't long before the book slid to the floor and Dix fell asleep.

Dix hadn't set the alarm for this morning, and he woke up late, just past seven a.m. He did a quick shave and shower and dressing and drove to work, arriving just before eight.

He checked for messages, and then checked the booking sheets from last night. Fortunately, he did not recognize any names. The he went into the coffee room for a cup of coffee and a pastry. Someone always brought in an assortment of pastries.

Catherine was sitting at the far end of the conference table having coffee and reading the morning paper. She looked up at Dix, and she saw something in his expression that made her give him a questioning look. *He's up to something*, she thought.

Dix took his coffee and pastry and sat down across the table from Catherine. She was wearing a muted green plaid business style suit and a dark green box hat.

"Morning, Catherine."

"Morning, Dix," she replied. Then she looked directly at him with that same questioning look. "You look like a man with a heavy load that you want to share."

"Is it that obvious?" asked Dix.

"It is to me, but then I'm not one to pry unless you would feel better sharing it."

"You are right, Catherine. I would feel better sharing, but I can't tell you very much. Just between you and me and the conference table, I am caught up in a situation that is going to involve a confrontation with our favorite narc. If all goes well, I'll be back in the office by four p.m. with no more shadows to worry about."

"Are you talking about a terminal confrontation?" Catherine asked, with a note of concern in her voice.

"It will be terminal, but not in the sense of being life ending for anyone. At least that's the plan."

"And if all does not go as planned?" asked Catherine.

"You know what they say about the 'best laid plans of mice and men.'" Dix replied. "There are always consequences of every action, both intended and unintended. We just hope to control both."

"Who's *we*?" Dix.

"I can't elaborate on that. Suffice it to say that I will be leaving here about noon and returning about four. If I come back smiling, you know all is well and I'll give you the details. And Catherine..."

"Yes?"

"Mums the word."

"Of course.

At about noon, Dix left the department, checked out a county car and drove to the meeting location to wait for Armund. They were to meet just up the street from the entrance to the fairgrounds. The fair was still going on, but there were no horse racing on Friday, so the crowd and traffic were light. Dix parked the car just inside the fairground, in a parking place reserved for county officials. Unless someone saw him park, no one would know whose car it was.

Dix walked a half block up from the fairground gate, leaned against the cyclone fence, and waited.

The wait was longer than Dix had expected and he found himself pacing up and down the sidewalk, constantly looking down the street for any sign of Armund's car. It was a hot day, and heat waves seemed to radiate off of the sidewalk wherever Dix stood.

Finally, he heard a car honking and saw Armund pulling over to the curb and slowing down. He also saw Bozeman's old Chevy about six cars back. Dix dove head first through the open window of Armund's car and the two of them sped off down the street and drove out Linden Valley Road.

Armund drove fast, but not so fast as to lose Bozeman. After driving five miles, they turned up Ramona Mountain Road, and then up the long drive to Collins' house. Armund was certain that Bozeman had seen them turn up the drive, but they didn't know if he would follow them up immediately or wait and drive up quietly in a few minutes. Either way, they prepared for the confrontation.

Armund turned his car around to face out the drive- way and parked about twenty feet out from the house. He stood alongside the left fender of his car, laying his 12-gauge trench gun on the fender, covering it with a blanket he had taken from the car. His hand was under the blanket and resting on the trigger guard.

Dix stood even with the front of Armund's car and about twenty feet to the right. He carried a Beretta M9 in an open holster on his side. Holly stood in the shadows alongside the house and far to the right of Dix, rifle in hand and at the ready. They had each put on a vest made of spider silk, with pockets for inserting ceramic plates, that Dix was told would deflect a bullet.

The air was still except for an occasional light gust that filtered through the trees and sent an array of bay leaves raining to the ground. It was quiet. They waited.

After about five minutes they heard a car coming up the drive, and coming fast. It turned the corner and drove onto the flat area, stopping twenty feet from where Dix was standing. Bozeman and Simmons both exited their car and walked to the front.

"What the hell are you two doing here?" commanded Dix.

"I knew you were into it," replied Bozeman. "You and your friends think you are going to cut me out of the trade. Well, think again."

"We're going to cut you out of it, all right, Bozeman. And we are not like those two punks you shot up in Windsor."

"Who are you talking about?"

"You know, those two guys with the drug lab you two raided, and then shot, and then tried to rig it like a shootout with those throw-away guns you planted on them at the scene."

"Those two punks had it coming, and they didn't know what hit them," said Simmons. "Anyone who tries to move into our territory gets the same."

"But why did you have to kill them?" Dix asked.

"Because we could. It was easy and we enjoyed it, just like we're going to do with you."

Then it all happened within thirty seconds. Simmons drew his .45 cal. pistol and shot Dix twice in the chest. Both bullets hit him within two inches of where his heart would be. Before Simmons could get off a third shot, Armund raised his trench gun and let go with two blasts. The 12-guage shot spread Simmons all over the side of their car, and he was dead before he had another thought.

At almost the same time, Bozeman reached for his pistol, but Holly fired one shot into Bozeman's right shoulder. Bozeman was spun around by the impact, his pistol went flying, and his arm was held onto his shoulder by some flesh and a bone or two. He grabbed his shoulder and fell to the ground screaming.

Holly stepped out into the yard and went over to Bozeman. She quickly searched him and removed a snub-nosed .38 from his ankle holster, and then picked up his other gun where it had fallen. "You are under arrest, Mr. Bozeman. Sorry that your friend over there is no longer available to achieve the same status."

Bozeman looked over to where Simmons lay dead. "Well, at least he got in the last lick on Monroe. I saw his bullets hit right on the mark." Bozeman grimaced and grinned at the same time.

Dix lay sprawled on the ground after he had been shot. Holly ran to him. The impact of Simmon's shots had knocked Dix off his feet. Armund and Shoenfield joined Holly and they all stared down at Dix and then at each other.

Dix didn't move.

"Oh, my God, Holly, do you know his next of kin, or of any relatives we need to contact?" asked Armund.

"I think we really need to get him some help," said Holly.

One of the agents radioed several other members of the task force that were waiting nearby. Within two minutes an ambulance and a tow truck came up the drive and onto the scene. One medical technician gave immediate treatment to Bozeman's shoulder wound. He said that he needs more attention than they could give on the scene and that he needed a hospital. The second medic went to assist with Dix.

Two additional CBI agents were in the tow truck, in addition to the driver and his helper.

Before Bozeman's car was towed to impound, the two agents inventoried the contents. Seven pistols and two shotguns were found in the trunk, in addition to drugs and narcotics. The car would be impounded in the police lot in Sacramento.

Chapter Twenty-Eight

The medic checked Dix and said that his breathing was normal. Holly and Armund smiled at each other and looked back down at Dix.

He still didn't move.

"I guess we'll just have to bury him here, just as he is," Holly said loudly.

Dix still didn't move.

Holly nudged him in the ribs with the toe of her shoe.

Dix still didn't move.

Holly knelt down alongside Dix and gently slapped his left cheek. "Come on, Dix. It's all over. You can wake up now."

Dix stirred, groaned, and slowly opened his eyes. Then he managed to speak, "What the hell...What happened?"

"You mean you were really out?" asked Holly.

As Dix sat up, Holly saw a splotch of blood on the back of his head. "Dix, you're bleeding."

The medic and Holly helped Dix stand and they walked him over to the ambulance, where the medic saw that Dix had a nasty cut and bump on the back of his head. The impact of being shot knocked him back. He had stumbled and fallen backwards and hit his head on an old gnarly root of one of those madrone trees. The medic cleaned and dressed the cut, and then gave Dix a quick test for possible concussion.

The medic addressed Holly: "Your friend seems a little groggy, but he knows where he is, his eyes look clear, he has no loss of memory, and he doesn't feel nauseated. He seems okay, but he should get a full medical checkup as soon as possible just to be sure."

Holly noticed that the two bullets fired by Simmons were still lodged in the protective vest Dix was wearing. She pointed to them and said, "Good thing we had you wear that vest, or you would be dead right now."

Dix took off the vest and opened his shirt. The bullets had left two impressions on his chest that looked like bruises. Dix touched them and winced. He was tender there. He smiled at Holly. "Thanks for the vest."

The medic applied disinfectant and an antibiotic salve to the two bruises and covered them with small adhesive pads, telling Dix that they would heal within a week.

The medic got into the ambulance, along with the other one and the driver, and two CBI agents, and they left the scene.

Dix looked around at all the agents and at Bozeman's car and the tow truck. He finally noticed Simmons. Most of him was lying alongside the car. They were covering him with a canvas. He also noticed an older man wearing a suit and tie who seemed to be in the center of everything, directing some of the movements.

"Holly, it looks as though I have missed all the action. I can truly say that I didn't sign up for this. I need to change my lifestyle. Regardless, fill me in on what happened and where we are in all this."

Holly described to Dix what had occurred from the moment he was shot by Simmons until now. "Simmons is dead, as you saw, but we got Bozeman and their confessions of what occurred in that Windsor shootout. He'll be housed in the jail in Sacramento after he is discharged from the hospital there. They'll keep him in protective custody, and they hope to have the venue moved there for trial as well. That man over there," and she pointed to the man in the suit, "is Bernard Chastain, Assistant Attorney General. He is here to make sure we did everything legally. He will be the state's prosecutor in the case."

Just as Holly was finished relating the events to Dix, Chastain walked over to them. He offered his hand and introduced himself to Dix. "Everything seems to be wrapped up here. Bozeman was taken to the hospital, and his vehicle was inventoried and towed. Armund and the other two agents will tidy up here and pay Mr. Collins and Mr. Shoenfield for their time and trouble. I want to thank you for all your help, Dix. You provided the perfect setup location and offered yourself as bait. I'm glad you weren't hurt any more seriously."

"Thank you and all these agents for pulling off the perfect trap and arrest. I do regret that Simmons won't be around to face trial, but I am thrilled that Bozeman will receive his full due."

The door to the house opened and Shoenfield and Collins came out once they saw that the scene was secure. They walked over and met with Dix and Holly.

"Dix," continued Chastain, "I understand that you plan to recommend to the court that Mr. Shoenfield's probation be terminated and that his record be expunged. I'll write an official letter to the court in support of that. Give Holly the details about to whom I should write to, and I'll see that it is taken care of."

"That will put the icing on the cake, Mr. Chastain. Now we can all get back to business."

"One final task I have to perform while I'm here" Chastain said, "is to meet with the sheriff and explain what has occurred under his not-so-watchful-eye. Holly is going with me. Do you care to join us? You might be able to fill him in on some details about Bozeman and Simmons that he should know."

"It would be my pleasure to join you. And you should have Captain Barnett, Bozeman's supervisor, present at the same time. He is the one who let Bozeman and Simmons free to run amok."

Dix said goodbye to Armund and the other agents, and told Shoenfield that he would be in touch. Then he joined Chastain and Holly, as they drove into town to visit with Sheriff Kentfield.

They entered the reception area of the sheriff's department, and Chastain went to the counter to request to meet with the sheriff. They were greeted by a civilian counter person. "May I help you," she asked.

"Here is my card. I am Bernard Chastain, Assistant Attorney General of California. I need to speak with the sheriff."

"May I tell him what this is in regard to?" responded the clerk.

"No, you may not. Just tell his office that it is an urgent matter that requires his immediate attention. Do you understand? Immediate attention, as in now?"

"Yes, I understand. It will just be a minute."

Chastain turned to Dix and Holly and grinned. They stood there waiting for the sheriff.

"He really enjoys his position of authority," said Holly.

"Yes, I can see that he does," responded Dix.

Within two minutes a side door opened and a deputy beckoned them inside. "I'll take you to the sheriff. Please follow me."

They followed the hallway to the rear of the building, took an elevator two flights up, and then walked down the hall and stopped at the door marked, Sheriff Kentfield – Private. The deputy knocked and then opened the door and escorted them inside. The sheriff was a large-framed man of about fifty, with a ruddy complexion and gray crew cut hair. He looked to be in good physical condition.

Sheriff Kentfield rose and introductions were made all around. "I'm from the Office of the Attorney General, as you can see by my card. Holly Trent is a Special Agent with the State Bureau of Narcotic Enforcement, and I think you know Dix Monroe, from the probation department."

Just then the door opened and Captain Barnett entered the room. Chastain re-introduced everyone to him. Barnett took a seat to the side of the sheriff's desk, where the sheriff had directed him.

"Now what is this all about?" asked the Sheriff.

"This is about two of your deputies, Bozeman and Simmons, who were allegedly under the supervision of Captain Barnett. Aside from their official duties, they were involved in drug distribution, extortion, and murder. We confronted them a short time ago with the intent of making arrests. We did arrest Bozeman, after he was shot and disarmed, and Simmons was shot and killed after he shot and attempted to kill Monroe. You will find him in your morgue as we speak. Bozeman has been taken to a hospital for treatment to his shoulder and will then be transported to jail in Sacramento, where he will be kept in solitary confinement for his own protection."

Captain Barnett's face turned bright red and he seemed to shrivel up in the chair. The sheriff had a shocked expression.

"Why wasn't I notified by your office before any action was taken against my deputies?" demanded the sheriff.

"The way those deputies were allowed to run roughshod over this county, committing crimes at will, led us to believe that we could not trust your office. For all we knew, you might tell Captain Barnett and he might warn them. We took Bozeman to Sacramento and planned to request a change of venue for trial proceedings for the same reason. And my dear sheriff, after we leave here, I am referring the matter to the grand jury. I am requesting an investigation of your department and its management structure and level of accountability for your staff."

The sheriff puffed up and tried to act shocked and indignant. "I am shocked by all the events you have told me. We had no idea. A referral to the grand jury is not necessary. I can assure you that we can handle this within house, and I will see to it that all are held accountable."

"You should have been doing that right along. That is all I have to say. Thank you for your time."

Chastain, Holly, and Dix rose in unison and exited the room.

"I think that we should explain the situation to your chief in the probation department. And then you should follow the medic's suggestion and take a few days off in order to have a complete physical and to allow those bruises to heal," stated Chastain.

All three walked over to the probation department and entered by the front door. Chastain said that he and Holly would wait in the lobby, while Dix saw that it was convenient to meet with the chief.

Dix walked down the hall and knocked on the chief's door.

"Come in," responded Chief Clausen. The assistant chief, James Bunting, was in there as well.

"I have Bernard Chastain, from the state's attorney general office and this is Holly Trent from the Bureau of Narcotic Enforcement. They would like to have a few minutes of your time to explain a situation we all were in today."

"By all means," replied Clausen. Have them come right back here."

Dix went to the lobby and returned with Chastain and Holly and led them into the chief's office. All eyes of the deputies in the room were fixed on the parade.

There wasn't sufficient room for everyone to sit, and Clausen offered to move them to the conference room. Chastain, however, said it wasn't necessary and that they would not be there very long. He then proceeded to give Clausen and Bunting the details of the morning's actions.

Clausen was surprised and seemed spellbound with Chastain's narration. Bunting sat there calmly, showing only an occasional smile. Both glanced at Dix from time to time.

When Chastain was through talking, Bunting commented that this incident will naturally be reported in the press, and there will be rumors flying about the justice complex. He suggested that it would be useful if all the deputies currently in the office convened, with Chastain, Holly, and Dix, for a similar explanation. They need to know the story firsthand before the rumors start.

All agreed, and everyone was assembled in the conference room, where Chastain, Holly, and Dix repeated the details of the action. You could have heard a pin drop when Chastain finished. Everyone looked at Dix. He smiled, shrugged his shoulders, and then winked at Catherine.

Chastain also said that he would be setting up an office in an area suggested by Dix in order to take witness statements from any probationers who had personal knowledge of Bozeman's actions. Dix would also arrange for any deputies having those probationers to assist in escorting them to and from that office.

When all was said and done, Chastain and Holly said their goodbyes and walked toward the rear door. Before Dix could leave, Clausen, Bunting, and all the deputies gathered around him, shook his hand and congratulated him on such a heroic action. Catherine gave him a big hug and then punched him on the shoulder.

Dix was told to take the rest of the week off on sick leave to attend to any treatment needs and to recuperate.

Chastain and Holly drove Dix back toward the fair- ground so that he could get his car. Dix thanked them for all they did and arranged a time for them to contact each other to follow the procedure with Bozeman through to the end. Holly gave Dix a hug and a kiss on the cheek. "I have missed you, Dix. Give me a call."

He returned the county car to the garage and drove home in his own car. He turned his mind to what lay ahead.

What am I going to tell Cluny?

Chapter Twenty-Nine

Dix and Cluny had agreed that she would come to his house at six p.m.; she would bring the entrée, and Dix would prepare a salad. This would be their evening alone.

Dix thought to himself, ready or not, *tonight is the night*. He had planned to ask Cluny for her hand in marriage. He made sure that he had the ring readily available. He showered and shaved for the second time that day and put on a fresh shirt.

Dix prepared a Caesar salad, with small slices of baked chicken and a Caesar dressing. He set the table and opened a bottle of *Pinot Noir* so it could breathe, and be ready for a toast to their happiness.

A few minutes before six, Dix heard Cluny's car drive up and park. He opened the door and watched her walk to the door. He also saw Billy run next door to his grandparents house.

Cluny was carrying a covered dish that must be hot because she was holding it with mitts. She walked through the door, gave Dix a quick kiss, and headed for the kitchen. She put the dish down on the counter and then turned on the oven to warm, placing the hot dish inside on the rack.

Cluny turned and met Dix in the middle of the living room, and they exchanged a long, wet kiss. The pressure of her body on his chest pushed in on the bruises left by the bullet marks and, although he tried not to, he winced slightly and pulled back from her just enough to relieve the pressure.

Cluny sensed his discomfort, pulled back from his embrace, and asked, "Dix, is there a problem?"

"No, it's just that I have a small bruise there," and he placed his fingers over his chest where the bruises were.

"Oh, I'm sorry. I didn't know. May I see?"

"No, it's nothing, really. I don't want to make a fuss over it. And I don't want to break the mood."

"Are we in a mood?" Cluny asked.

"Well, I wanted to create one before we do anything else, Cluny. Stand right there."

Dix removed the ring box from his front pocket, took one of Cluny's hands in his, and opened the ring box and knelt in front of her. "Cluny Ramm, will you be my wife?"

Cluny stood there momentarily stunned, and then grinned from ear to ear, took the ring out of the box, and moved to embrace and kiss Dix. Then she was aware again of the bruised area on Dix's chest, and she hesitated and pulled back.

"Dix, if we are going to be physical with each other tonight, I need to know about that bruise. Where is it? How did you get it? Please share that with me."

Dix realized that the events of the evening would not move forward until Cluny was satisfied. He knew that once she had her mind set on something, that it had to be settled before anything else was going to happen. She was both stubborn and determined.

Dix opened his shirt and showed Cluny the two bruises that were still covered with adhesive pads. She looked at them and then at him, but said nothing. Dix knew that she wasn't satisfied, so he gently pulled on the pads and revealed the two marks.

"My God, Dix. How did you get those?"

He hesitated, not wanting to tell her of the events with Bozeman, but he knew that she would press him until he told her. He was learning that much about her already. He also knew that her feelings were hers, and that he would never be able to create anything different just to suit himself.

"Okay, Cluny, have a seat and I'll explain it all to you."

They sat on the couch, turning to face each other, and Dix related in detail the entire story of him and Bozeman. When he got to the part that described being shot by Simmons and falling to the ground and hitting his head on that gnarly tree root, Cluny moved back and curled on the couch and placed her left hand over her mouth. She took on a frightened look that increased in intensity as Dix talked on, and tears formed in her eyes.

When he was through talking, Cluny stared at him and then said, "Oh, my God, Dix. Oh, my God. You could have been killed."

"But I wasn't," Dix replied.

"But you could have...Oh, Dix what have you done? I...I can't...I can't live with the idea that you might be killed...that you might be taken from me. I can't ..." And she began to sob.

Dix reached for her to hold her, but she pushed his arms away. She took the ring he had given her and placed it on the couch near him. She rose, grabbed her coat, and ran out the door, still crying.

Dix stood and watched her run out of the house and down the stairs. He didn't hear her car start, so he assumed that she went next door to her parents' house. He had never felt so frustrated in his life. He realized, before he told her about the scene with Bozeman, that it was bad timing; that where was no nice way out of this. She would not let up until he explained how he came by those bruises.

Dix was angry with himself for not handling the situation better, and he was angry with Cluny for reacting the way she did. Cluny carried so much baggage since her husband died because, as she felt it, he abandoned her. The thought of being abandoned by Dix was more that she could handle. He saw that now. Yet what was he supposed to do? There was no sense telling her to be reasonable because feelings don't listen to reason. He couldn't keep things from her, and he wasn't about to change jobs just to please her.

The more Dix thought about the situation, the more angry he became at Cluny. It was not what he did that created the scene. It was her reaction to what he did and what might have happened.

Dix began to see the situation as one impossible to correct. No matter what he said or did, she will still feel apprehensive and, knowing that, he would feel in a double bind, blamed by her for her feelings, and angry at her for having them. There was nothing that he could do or say to change the situation, and why should he have to anyway? That was on her, and yet he knew that she would resent him if she sensed that he felt that way. And yet her fragile emotions tugged at him and he wanted to be there for her. But how far could he go in carrying her baggage?

It was a classic "catch twenty-two" situation, and Dix saw no way out. Now he realized how relevant that Jacque Brel song that Cluny's mother shared with her and she shared with him was. *Ne me quitte pas* – Don't leave me. And Dix had responded, *Jamias* –Never.

Has *never* already come and gone?

Saturday and Sunday came and went, and Dix heard nothing from Cluny. Every time a car drove by and slowed down, Dix went to the window and looked out, hoping it would be her. Several times he thought of driving out to her house and talking to her and trying to work it out, but he didn't. He didn't know what to work out.

He woke up a little after seven a. m. Monday morning, got up, dressed for a morning run, and drove to the high school, parking near the entrance to the track as always. He did his usual slow warmup lap and then ran flat out for eight laps. Afterwards he lay on the football field gasping for air. Then he drove home.

After a shave, shower, and breakfast, Dix decided that he needed someone with whom to talk over his situation. He phoned the probation department and asked for Catherine.

She picked up her phone: "Catherine Williams here."

"Hi, Catherine. It's me, Dix. Don't say my name."

"Well, hello, there," Catherine responded with a tone somewhere between sarcasm and humor. "What shall we talk about?"

"I'm in a situation and I need to talk with someone who will listen and respond without judgment. I figured you for that."

"I'm not sure if that is flattery or fawning, but I'm all ears."

"Can we meet somewhere?"

"Where are you now?"

"I'm at home."

"I am leaving work early today, on my way to San Francisco. I'm staying with a friend for the overnight, and we're going to see the San Francisco Symphony, featuring a young Japanese conductor, Seiji Ozawa as guest conductor. They are playing Mussorgsky's *Pictures at an Exhibition*, so I can meet you in or near Riverton."

"That's more information than I needed to know, Catherine, but I do appreciate you sharing your cultural indulgence. Anyway, there is a Denny's restaurant just off the freeway at the first exit into town. We could meet there. What's a good time for you?"

"One o'clock is good."

"See you there. Lunch is on me."

Dix arrived early at Denny's and sat in a corner booth from where he could see everyone who entered, stayed, and left. Catherine was right on time. She spotted Dix as soon as she entered and went to his table.

"Hi, Dix. You look anxious. How do you feel?"

"Catherine, I am about a thousand miles from no- where. I thank you for meeting me."

Dix gave Catherine the complete rundown on the situation with him and Cluny.

The waitress took their order. Patty melts and house salad for each. Catherine had coffee and Dix just had water.

"Dix, it sounds as though there was poor timing with your proposal to Cluny, followed by the description of the shootout with Bozeman and Simmons. And yet, it probably is good that it happened in that sequence. If you had told her about the shootout, she would have left without ever knowing about your proposal. Now that she knows, the ball is in her court, so to speak. If she really loves you and wants to marry you, she will have to make the first move to settle things. It all depends on how strongly she is hung up on the idea of losing you. For her it is a pleasure-pain dichotomy, and I don't see anything that you can do to ease the situation."

"I feel so helpless," said Dix. "You know me. I'm not the kind to sit around and wait for things to happen. I have always been able to assert myself and resolve problems."

"Are you sure that you want this to be resolved? If she is unable to sort it out, she will break it off and you will be free to move forward."

"Two weeks ago, I was thinking that the last thing I needed in my life was a woman. But now I don't want to move forward without her."

"Are you certain of that? Have you thought it through to that possibility?"

"I have, but then I see her left in pain and loss, and I want to be there to help her."

"Well, that reminds me of what my dad told my brother when he reached age eighteen and graduated high school. He told him that it was time for him to get off the wagon. He was too old to be carried."

"I just want to be there for her when she needs me. We'll need each other."

"I think that Cluny has a lot of baggage to carry," said Catherine.

"I can help her carry it from time to time, if she'll let me."

"Dix, I don't think she wants to feel dependent on someone else. She needs to stay strong and independent. In fact, she might overdo that a little."

"She has been on her own for several years and has had to carry all her own weight and that of her son. She needs to stay strong to keep that going."

"I know where you are going with this, Dix. You need her as much as you think she needs you, and you hope to work it out that way. Remember, you might have to deal with her emotional conflicts and moods again from time to time. Are you ready for that?"

"I am, Catherine. I really am."

"Then you might also accept some responsibility for this plight that has been created. You wooed her and pursued her, and then told her you loved her. That got her to drop her guard, and then you had sex with her. The two of you were committed. She expected this wonderful world to be her's forever. Then you threw a shootout into the mix and shattered the illusion. She will have to create a more realistic world view and come to you. And you you are committed now, and might find it impossible to back out if your feelings change. You're committed to her, to her son, and to her parents, and there would be no easy way out."

"I would never want a way out, Catherine. I'm in this for the long haul. She is the one that I want to create a life with. You know what they say, *for better or worse*. Well, we can always make it better."

"I hear you, Dix, and I know the two of you will make it together. Love, and the desire to stay married is all it takes.

"I want to thank you for listening to me and sharing your perspective, Catherine. I'm not sure that we resolved anything, but I think I have a better understanding of where we are and how I feel."

"I have always believed that things work themselves out the way they are supposed to be. Just be there as it happens. And Dix, she is a lucky girl. If I were twenty years younger, I would be after you myself. But don't get me wrong. You're far from perfect, and you have some baggage too, and she will help you carry it if you let her. I think that you need her as much as she needs you."

"Catherine, I appreciate your candor. For Cluny and me it won't be like the lame leading the blind. Just two people in love, trying to make it to the end of the day. You are a great friend to have, Catherine."

They laughed and both rose from the table. They shared a long hug, and then went their separate ways.

Chapter Thirty

The fog crept over the hills during the night and shrouded Riverton and the Santa Inez River that flowed from San Francisco Bay through the town of Riverton. Of course, the river was actually a tidal estuary that snaked north from San Pablo Bay to Riverton and wandered north a few miles, as it narrowed to the flats, where it was fed by small streams from the nearby hills.

It had been called a creek for many years until the state declared it a river, and a navigable river at that. Before the coming of the train, it had been the main commercial access from the Bay area to Riverton and points north, carrying agricultural produce and raw materials to the Bay area aboard sailing scows, or scow schooners, as they were called.

The River Trail began at the southern edge of town on the east side of the river and ran parallel to the river for ten miles across fields and alongside several marshes where bird watching was a common pastime. It was a dirt trail cleared by a small bulldozer and maintained by the many feet that trod on it over the years.

It was seven-thirty am when Dix parked his vehicle at the trailhead parking lot to begin his Saturday morning run. Not his usual activity. He strapped on a small fanny pack that contained his wallet and a Ruger .380, just in case. He placed a water bottle in the pocket on the side of the pack.

Dix took the first mile at an easy trot, and then began a serious run. He thought he might run until the sadness left him. The way he felt now he just wanted to keep running.

Ducks bobbed on the ripples in the marshes created by breezes that came and went. An occasional egret stood motionless at the edge of the marsh, poised to capture breakfast. The red-winged blackbirds were performing their balancing acts while perched on the sides of the marsh reeds.

At the five-mile mark, Dix paused and sat on a memorial bench dedicated to one of the local birdwatchers. He took a long drink from his water bottle. He watched as a small tug came around a bend in the river and passed him by, towing a barge loaded with ground oyster shells meant for the chicken ranches located in the town's rural areas. The only sounds were the purring of the tugboat's Gray Marine diesel engine and the lapping of the river against the barge. Dix exchanged waves with a man in the tugboat's pilot house. After that it was peaceful. Absolutely quiet. *Will my life ever be like this?* he asked.

After a few minutes a man came walking along the trail toward Dix. He wore street clothes, a red-and-black wool shirt and white sneakers, and carried a large camera on a tripod. He looked to be in his mid-fifties or early sixties, balding on top, with a ring of gray hair around the fringe. Dix thought at first that the man was a birdwatcher looking for a good viewing spot. However, he held the camera in his left hand and had his right hand inside his jacket pocket. He wasn't looking at any of the marshes, but instead seemed to be looking at Dix. His gaze never strayed. The memory of Bozeman came to mind. Could this man be a narc as well? Maybe a dealer looking to get even with Dix. Dix, always hoping for the best but always being prepared for the worst, slid his fanny pack around so that the pack faced front. He slowly unzipped the pack and slipped his hand around the Beretta .380 nestled at the bottom.

As the man got near, it became evident that he was going to sit down on the bench next to Dix. Dix slid to the right end of the bench so that the man would be sitting on his left. That way the man would find it awkward to pull something out of his right coat pocket. Dix wondered if he was being cautious or had he graduated to paranoia.

The man sat down and smiled and nodded. As he sat, his body slumped and he let out a big sigh. "Looks like the fog is lifting."

"Yes," replied Dix, "it's going to be a nice day."

"Jinx is my name," offered the man. "Jinx Faraday. I came out here to photograph some birds, but not having much luck in finding any."

"My name is Dix," he replied. "Not many here except herons, egrets, and those redwing blackbirds this time of year. Nice camera."

"I guess so. I don't know how to use one like this."

"Is it your camera?"

"No. It belongs to the place where I live. I saw it lying on the table this morning, so I thought I would bring it along with me."

"Do they know that you borrowed it?"

"I don't know. I never asked."

"Where do you live, Jinx?"

"I'm not sure. Somewhere in town."

It finally occurred to Dix that Jinx was suffering from memory loss and maybe even Alzheimer's, and had just wandered off.

"Jinx, can I help you find your way back home?"

"No thanks. I'll think I'll sit here for a while and then walk back."

"Are you going to be okay?"

"Oh sure. I come out here often."

The man started to pull his right hand out of his pocket. It held something. Dix tensed slightly. The hand was out and it held a sack of Bull Durham and rolling paper.

"Mind if I have a smoke?" he said.

"Sure. Help yourself."

"I don't know how to smoke. I took this from the store yesterday, but I don't know how to use it."

Jinx was confused, but didn't seem to mind. "Here, let me hold that for you. Maybe later I can show you how to use it."

"Okay. I like sitting here. It's so peaceful."

"It is. Life can get complicated sometimes. Too many things happening at the same time."

"That never happens to me, Dix. I don't remember much, so there's not much happening with me, so it doesn't get complicated for me."

Dix thought it interesting that Jinx remembered his name, and was aware that he usually didn't remember things. Somehow, he was aware of his own condition. Dix could see how that could be an advantage. If one could just shut off the world when he wanted to. *I'd like to do that right now*, he mused. But then he accepted the idea that dealing with life's issues is a part of living.

"If you're going to be all right, I need to keep up my pace before I cool off." Dix rose from the bench. "Nice talking to you, Jinx. Have a good day." And he trotted down the path toward the end.

When he had finished his run and got back to his car, he planned to locate a phone and call the local police to see if anyone had reported Jinx missing.

As Dix approached the parking area at the end of the trail, he saw a sheriff's patrol car. The deputy was just coming out of the portable toilet. He walked to his car and stood there waiting for Dix to reach him.

"Morning Officer," said Dix. "It looks like you're waiting for someone." *Is he waiting for me?* Dix wondered.

"I am, in a way. Got a report of a man who walked away from the Cardinal House. The Alzheimer's care facility at the edge of town."

"What did he look like?"

"About sixty. Faded black slacks, a red-and-black wool shirt and white sneakers. Wasn't wearing a hat.

"I sat with him for a few minutes at the bench five miles back. I expect he's on his way to the other end. He seemed sociable and in control of his facilities to some degree, but obviously having memory lapses. He was in no hurry to get anywhere."

"If you don't mind leading me back, I think that this trail can handle my car."

"Sure, whatever I can do." Dix got in the passenger side of the sheriff's car. When they were both seated, he offered his hand and said, "I'm Dix Monroe."

"I'm Bill Tankard," replied the deputy. "Monroe, huh. That name is familiar. How would I know that name?" asked the deputy, as he started driving on the trail heading toward where Jinx might be.

"I'm a deputy probation officer. Have been for a few months. I was an investigator for the DA's office before that."

"Aha! You must be the guy who had that shootout with those narcs Bozeman and Simmons"

"I'm the one. Just a misunderstanding on their part. How did you know about that?"

"Word gets around. Can't keep something like that a secret. I'd like to have been there to see it happen. But let me tell you. You did the entire department a favor. Those were bad cops, out of control, and needed to be stopped."

"So, I've been told. I appreciate you sharing those sentiments with me."

They had driven about five miles when they saw Jinx sitting on the bench where Dix had left him. He stood up and looked frightened when he saw the car driving toward him. He started to run away down the trail. It was more of a waddle than a run.

"Let me get out here," said Dix. "I think I can approach him better on foot and talk him into coming with us."

Dix trotted up the trail toward Jinx and called for him to wait up. He and Jinx walked together for fifty feet or so until Dix calmed him and made him feel safe getting into the car. They followed the trail to its beginning, where Dix had parked. He left Jinx in the good care of the deputy. Dix bid farewell, and they went their separate ways.

Dix decided that he had run enough for the day and drove home.

Chapter Thirty-One

As he drove up to his house, he saw Cluny's car parked in front of her parents' house. *Did she come into town to see them or to see me?* he wondered. *Maybe she is inside my house now waiting to talk.* He had not locked the door.

He entered his house slowly and looked around, wondering and hoping. He called out once. No response. He felt a little let down, but still kept his hope alive that they would talk at some point today. Why else would she come into town?

Dix shaved, showered, and dressed in denim shorts, a plaid cotton tee-shirt, and flip flops. He put several Artie Shaw records from the 1940s on the phonograph. He listened to the first song, Cole Porter's "Softly, as in a Morning Sunrise," and then he went into the kitchen and started the coffee.

Before it was ready to drink, someone knocked on the front door. Dix turned and saw through the curtain that it was Cluny. His heart leaped and his stomach churned, and he tried to neutralize his anxiety.

Dix opened the door. "Hi, Dix."

"Come in, Cluny."

She walked over to the lounge chair and sat down. Dix sat on the couch across from her. Ironically, Artie Shaw's rendition of the Gershwin song, "Love Walked Right In," began playing.

Cluny sat there taking a few deep breaths, as if she was working up the courage to speak. Dix sat there patiently waiting. This was her gig. Finally, she looked directly at Dix and began talking.

"Dix, I...I'm not sure where to begin."

"What did you come here to say, Cluny?"

"Dix, I know that I was very emotional and reacted strongly at your story of being shot, and possibly, I over-reacted. I came to apologize and to talk about it. I hope I haven't made a mess of us."

"Do you still want there to be an *us*, Cluny?"

"Yes, I want *us*. I need *us*. After a long talk with my parents and a long process of thinking about everything, about *us*, I think that I have put *us* in perspective."

"What was your mother's take on all this? Did she quote some more French songs for you?"

"No. No more French songs."

And they smiled at each other. That was a start.

"Actually, my dad spoke up and quoted two lines from two poems, and then we talked about how they applied to my life."

"I'm curious to know which poems." said Dix

In Memoriam, by Tennyson was the first one. The lines that applied went like this:

> 'Tis better to have loved and lost
> Than never to have loved at all.

"I know now that I never did have love before. I felt abandoned by my husband when he was killed in the war. But we had never learned to love. I felt cheated and alone because I have so much love to share and couldn't. Over the years, I have come to terms with that part of my life. Now, I have found you, my love, and I don't want to lose you, but no matter what the future holds, I will always have you."

"And the second poem?" inquired Dix.

"The second poem was a sonnet by Edna St. Vincent Millay, "What Lips My Lips Have Kissed, And Where, And Why," which ended with these lines:

> I only know that summer sang in me
> A little while, that in me sings no more.

And summer sang in me, Dix, when you came into my life. Please don't let it stop singing. I love you so much."

Dix stood up and faced Cluny. She was crying and crying out to him. He held out his arms, and she melted into them, and they both were crying. They hugged for a very long time, neither wanting to let the other go.

Finally, they parted, and Cluny said, "Is there something that you want to ask me again?"

"Wait," responded Dix. "Wait right there. I want to do this right. The old-fashioned way."

Dix ran out of the house and ran next door, leaving Cluny standing there with her mouth open. The O'Brien's front door was open and through the screen door Dix could hear George and Jackie talking. He didn't bother to knock and walked right in and went to where he heard their voices, the dining room.

George, Jackie, and Billy were sitting at the table playing Monopoly. All three looked up as he entered the room.

"Dix," said Jackie, surprised to see him alone.

"I need to talk to you George, man to man." Dix feigned a serious look on his face and tone in his voice, but George understood that this was not really a serious moment.

"Sure, Dix. Speak right up so we can all hear."

"George, I want your permission to marry your daughter."

George broke into a warm smile. "Any other scallywags I know would have abandoned ship a long time ago, but you, Dix, did not. You are no scallywag. Dix, you are an honorable man, and I will die contented that Cluny is safe in your arms."

Then George did the unexpected. He rose from his chair and gave Dix a warm hug. Jackie immediately rose and hugged Dix as well, and kissed him on the cheek.

"Then do I have your blessing too Jackie?"

"Yes, and it's about damn time."

Dix looked down at Billy and said, "And Billy, is it okay if I marry your mother?"

"Sure, Dix. That'd be keen. Will I get to call you Dad?"

"Billy, I'd be honored if you would." And he gave Billy a hug.

"Folks, I haven't actually proposed yet, so I had better go and take care of that."

"Dix." Jackie called out

"Yes," replied Dix.

"Dinner at six o'clock."

They all laughed, and Dix went back to his house. While he was gone, Cluny had washed her face and run a comb through her hair. She was standing in the middle of the living room when he entered.

"Where did you go?"

"I went to ask your father for your hand in marriage. And your mother, and Billy."

"You're a silly guy, and what did he and they say?"

"George and Billy said yes, and your mother said yes too, and that it was about damn time."

"Well, Mr. Monroe, we better get to it," said Cluny.

Dix removed the ring box from a drawer in the coffee table where he had stashed it and faced Cluny.

Dix knelt in front of her and they exchanged smiles. "Cluny Ramm, will you be my wife?"

"Dix Monroe, yes I will. And it's about damn time."

They hugged and laughed and kissed and cried.

Then they moved to the bedroom, where the sweet love-making began.

Later, they lay there completely satisfied, but emotionally and physically spent. Cluny lay with her arm across Dix's chest and her leg across his thighs. She kissed him on the shoulder.

"What are you thinking," asked Dix.

"I was just thinking how much I love how you love me."

"Cluny?"

"Yes?"

"I'm just thinking about what has happened in our lives in two short weeks. We are ready to live our lives together, but we have so much more to learn about each other. And we now have several decisions to make about our lives together."

"Like what?" Cluny responded.

"Well, you know, our likes and dislikes, our moods, our feelings about things. Where we are going to live? Your house or mine? Your job. Children. All those little things."

"You mean like that weird music you listen to?"

"Weird! I listen to nothing but the finest jazz and classic ballads."

"That's what I mean." They laughed, and Cluny poked Dix in the ribs with her finger.

Dix got out of bed and put a record on the phonograph and it started to play. "Now just listen. This is a 1958 recording of Chet Baker singing the Warren and Gordon classic, "The More I See You, the More I Want You.""

Cluny said, "The voice is a little rough, but I like the words." She took a few of the song's closing words and asked, "So how do we carry this out "as the years go by?""

"Well, Cluny, I don't think life offers a plan. We hold tightly to each other and just jump into the river and follow where the current takes us.'

"That sounds wonderful to me. Loving and living our lives together. Where do we start?" asked Cluny.

"We'll start for real tomorrow. But right now, we start by taking a shower."

"And then what?"

"And then we go next door. Your mother said dinner at six."

Other Titles by the Author

Fiction

The ZORN Conspiracy

The Searching

Bound for Bodie

Non-fiction

Basic Criminal Procedures (two editions)

Basic Procedures for Mobile Notary Signing Agents

Criminal Procedures in California (five editions)

Corrections in California: an Introduction to Probation, Institutions & Parole (two editions)

Juvenile Procedures in California (seven editions)

Readings in the Administration of Justice

Readings in Correctional Casework & Counseling

About the Author

Ed Peoples is a professor emeritus of Criminal Justice at Santa Rosa Junior College, where he taught for twenty years, and he also taught eight years at San Jose State University. He has previously written and published four textbooks and two anthologies in the justice field. Now retired from teaching, Ed is devoting his creative efforts in developing the main characters in this novel into a series of detective and adventure stories for subsequent novels. He lives with his wife in a small village in northern California.